PROUD LADY

Astrid

PROUD LADY

GERTRUDE CROWNFIELD

Illustrated by Agnes Lehman

PHILADELPHIA
J. B. LIPPINCOTT COMPANY
NEW YORK   LONDON   CHICAGO

OTHER BOOKS BY GERTRUDE CROWNFIELD

CRISTINA OF OLD NEW YORK
STRONG HEARTS AND BOLD
THE DECREE
KING'S PARDON
TRAITOR'S TORCH
MISTRESS MARGARET
DIANTHA'S SIGNET RING
LONE STAR RISING
ANGELIQUE
ETC.

TO

J. JEFFERSON JONES

ILLUSTRATIONS

PROUD LADY

CHAPTER 1

Gunnar keeps us uneasy. Hotheaded, ready with his fists, one can never guess what he will be into next."

Astrid Nilsson brought the words out slowly, reluctantly, for she was very fond of her older brother. She would not have spoken them about Gunnar to anyone outside her family except Eric Helm, but he was Gunnar's staunch friend as well as hers and he would understand.

He knew Gunnar's nature as well as she did, and would be equally certain to make allowances for him.

She was seated on the edge of the dock which ran out near the sally-port of Fort Casimir into the waters of the Delaware River. Two miles and more across the river was the Jersey shore. Her eyes were fixed upon it absently, her thoughts being engaged with Gunnar.

Eric, who stood beside her on the dock, responded with quick sympathy. "I would not worry too much, Astrid," he advised quietly. "Gunnar's heart is of the best. He is as honest as the sun. He flares up against injustice or unfairness and does not count the cost. Yet I don't believe he will get into any serious trouble."

Astrid did not answer at once. She twisted one of her long flaxen braids in and out between her fingers. The breeze from the river played over her silky hair that peeped a little from under the edge of her close white cap, banded and sprinkled with embroidered flowers in many colors.

She wore the wide dark skirt, the full apron brilliantly striped, the low scarlet bodice, white puffed sleeves and guimpe of a Swedish girl. Her skin was fair. Her eyes, steadfast in their gaze, were blue as the skies of midsummer. Low shoes of braided birch bark, shapely and supple as the Swedes and Finns knew how to weave, met her scarlet hose at her trim ankles.

Her companion wore elkskin breeches, frieze jacket, linen shirt, blue woolen stockings, coarse leather shoes, and felt hat whose brim came low over his forehead. All were of Swedish cut.

When Governor Johan Printz brought the first shipload of colonists to the New World from Sweden in 1643, he bore with him express commands from the King of Sweden that in the Swedish and Finnish settlements along the Delaware River, Swedish manners, customs, and dress were to be preserved unchanged. A New Sweden in every sense of the word was to be formed there.

These orders had been strictly obeyed except for such slight changes as climate and unavoidable circumstances had demanded.

Swedish rule had prevailed under changing governors until Petrus Stuyvesant in 1651 had seized the lands in the name of Holland and built Fort Casimir. The Swedes regained power only to lose it once more to the Dutch for good and all in 1654. Then Dutch colonists arrived and, instructed by Stuyvesant, laid out the little town of New Amstel, close to Fort Casimir. Ten years later the English seized Dutch possessions north and south for James, Duke of York, and New Amstel became New Castle, and so remained.

Nevertheless, throughout these changes in government, and in spite of plunderings by the conquerors, the Swedes and Finns had managed to pursue their own modes of life, and had been allowed to keep their lands and homes, and to live in peace.

There were, however, among these Swedes and Finns, some who resented Governor Francis Lovelace's high-handed ways of administering justice and interfering with the course of it, of making laws to suit himself without the voice or vote of Council or the will of the people; of setting aside laws or abolishing them to suit his personal whim, of choosing or deposing judges as he pleased.

Astrid was not without some reason for her fears in regard to her brother. Gunnar Nilsson, barely twenty years old, was one of the restive spirits, and was growing ripe for rebellion. This had made Astrid speak to Eric as she had; this shadowed her blue eyes while her vision was fixed unseeing on the farther shore.

She was five years younger than Gunnar, but was steadier of head and nature than he. She shared her parents' anxieties concerning him. Inevitably it would go hard with Gunnar if he should come into open conflict with the law or with existing rule.

Thus far nothing had occurred to stir him to any act that would have brought him within the arm of the law, but he was bold and reckless, and never counted the cost when once he was aroused by injustice of any sort.

At present New Castle was quiet and he was busy in the fields with his father. Hence there would appear to be no immediate cause for Astrid's uneasiness.

Eric waited patiently until she should speak again, hoping that her common sense would assert itself and bid her not to run ahead in imagination to disasters which might never occur.

He was not disappointed. Astrid finally withdrew her gaze from the distant shore and smiled faintly up at him.

"I must not be foolish," she said. "Gunnar is in no trouble as yet. If he ever should be, then my parents and I must do what we can to help him out of it. For the present I will not worry."

"And I will do whatever I can to help, too. That you know already, Astrid." He offered the promise earnestly, as much for Astrid herself as for Gunnar. No one pleased him in looks and ways as Astrid did.

To no one else did he ever speak his mind and heart as freely.

"Of that we can always be certain, Eric," she returned warmly. "We have no truer friend than you." She rose from the wooden dock. "I must go home now for mother will be needing me."

They left the Strand together and walked briskly along Chestnut Street toward her father's farm, which lay to the left of the great Bouwerie Wood belonging to Peter Alrichs.

The distance to be covered was short. In a few minutes the two arrived at the substantial log house which Lars Nilsson had built before Gunnar was born. The dwelling, constructed of round timber with sloping roof, overhanging second story, dormer windows, a tall oddly shaped chimney topped by a sharply peaked hood, had a friendly look.

In such a house as this Lars had been born in Sweden. He was convinced that he could offer his young bride Ingeborg no better home than this counterpart when he brought her to it. Ingeborg had thought likewise and had never changed her mind.

Astrid paused at the door, her hand upon the latch. "Will you come in, Eric?" she asked.

"Not now, but sometime soon."

"Here your welcome always waits for you," she

told him, smilingly.

Eric whistled softly to himself as he went away. Astrid's assurance of welcome meant much to the nineteen-year-old motherless lad. His home was a smaller and far less comfortable log house. He spent his days, and often his nights, in working with his father, Anders Helm, a longshore fisherman.

CHAPTER II

The door closed behind Astrid and she was in the main room of the house. In this the cooking was done; here the family gathered to eat and sit, to work and to rest. Two built-in beds were on the farther side of the yawning fireplace. Lars and Ingeborg slept in one of these. Astrid and her little twin sisters, Karin and Kirsten, occupied the other. Brightly striped curtains of thick woolen stuff concealed the beds by day, and were drawn together at night in winter to keep out the cold.

Two small windows set in the wall opposite the fireplace and the beds lighted the big room but dimly. The leaping crackling fire, burning bravely in the fireplace, saved the room from gloom and filled it with homely cheer.

Ingeborg Nilsson, tall, fair haired, and serene faced, was throwing a woolen coat of her husband's over the high clothes rail which hung suspended by iron bars from the rough beams of the ceiling.

"Was the air good by the river?" she inquired complacently of her daughter.

"Sweet and cool and fresh," replied Astrid.

"It has given you rosy cheeks," commented her mother approvingly, adjusting Lars' coat carefully over the rail.

Astrid laughed blithely. "My cheeks are always red, mother."

"As they should be," said Ingeborg, and stepped to the brick oven to see how her loaves of bread were getting on.

Astrid followed, and was just in time to draw back from the embers a pot of water which was about to boil over. "Eric was down by the dock," she informed her mother. "He sails out tonight with his father and may be gone till morning."

"A fine lad that Eric," returned Ingeborg. "I feel toward him almost as if he were my own son. I wish Gunnar were as steady." She thrust a clean straw into a baking loaf to test it. "Not quite done," she pronounced, pushing back the loaf and closing the oven door.

With a gentle hand she shook her ample skirts free from the flaxen-haired twins, who had run to press against her by the oven and sniff the sweet odor of the hot bread.

"Play by the other side of the hearth," she bade them.

"With these pink and white pebbles I have brought you from the river," coaxed Astrid, producing a handful from the deep pocket which hung by her side.

The twins seized them with squeals of delight and plumped themselves down beside the hearth to examine them. Quaint little figures they were, scarcely more than infants, yet dressed in all respects as Astrid was, except that where her bodice was scarlet, theirs were pale blue. Tiny embroidered caps fitted their heads neatly, puffed sleeves stood crisp and full over their chubby arms.

Precisely alike in shape and feature, even their own mother could not have told these twins apart if Karin had not had a wee mole at the side of her left ear, while Kirsten's mole was just above her right eyebrow.

Astrid loved them tenderly. Four years earlier, on the day that they were born, her mother had said to her, "See, my daughter, these little ones shall be partly yours. You must help me to bring them up." Astrid had flushed with pride, accepted the charge gladly, and been faithful to it.

They played happily now with their pebbles and their Swedish dolls. Astrid fell to polishing the tin plates and wiping every speck of dust from the wooden plates and mugs decorated in glowing colors, which stood in rows on the high shelf above the door.

The big room was shining with cleanliness and fragrant with the smell of fresh bread and steaming rye porridge when Lars and Gunnar stepped in at dusk.

A tall broad-shouldered pair, they were plain of feature and blond, their skins reddened and roughened by exposure to sun and wind. Both had candid honest faces. Lars' showed a quiet self-control; Gunnar's betrayed his impulsive hasty nature.

Ingeborg put an enormous wooden bowl of hot porridge in the center of the bare table; Astrid set a small wooden bowl filled with milk at each person's place and beside it she laid a wooden spoon. Gunnar lifted the twins to a bench next Astrid's stool. She would see to it that they did not daub themselves with the porridge, nor drip milk upon their clothes.

As soon as Lars and Gunnar had washed their hands and faces, and smoothed their hair, they drew up to the table. Heads were bowed, grace was said, and the meal began and went forward simply.

Each person dipped his or her spoon into the great bowl in the middle of the table for every separate mouthful of porridge, and then into his or her own bowl for milk. That was the Swedish peasant fashion, and they held to it.

When the edge of Gunnar's hunger was dulled somewhat, he began to talk. "If only we had a Swedish governor," he spluttered, resting his spoon in his almost emptied bowl of milk, "we might have real satisfaction. Even the Dutch must have been better than these English."

Ingeborg smothered a sigh, and Astrid gave attention to Karin, who was tipping her spoonful of porridge dangerously.

Lars answered his son. "Well, what now, Gunnar?"

"Nothing in particular today," acknowledged Gunnar, reaching for another mouthful of rye porridge, "but there is almost always something wrong."

"Perhaps if you had been old enough in the days of the Dutch governors to understand how matters were going," laughed Lars, shrugging his shoulders, "you would have been free with your grumblings even then. The Dutch were not so bad after the first, for they let us keep our farms and follow our own ways for the most part. Petrus Stuyvesant, who laid out this town, called it New Amstel; the English when they took it named it New Castle, but the town itself is not so different after all."

Gunnar, resting his elbows on the table, looked as though that were difficult to believe.

Lars went on quietly. "Jacob Alrichs, the Dutchman, was in charge for only a few years, but he did a great deal in that time. Our log town hall, our bakehouse, our forge, our guardhouse at the fort, our brick kilns, were all due entirely to him. In his very first year he had a hundred buildings put up. He gave us our first wharf, too, down by Fort Casimir."

"But Hinoyossa, if what I have been told is the truth, was bad," contested Gunnar obstinately. "If we could have had Swedish rule, as we had in the beginning—"

Lars interrupted him good-naturedly. "There again you would have had plenty to say, my boy.

His Excellency, old Johan Printz, who was our first Swedish governor, and who brought us over from Sweden, was none too well liked. He allowed no one to cross his will, nor to gainsay him. Such a man as he was! Everybody must run to do his bidding instantly. He was obstinate as a mule. And what a temper! His daughter, Juffrou Armgart Printz, has the same; his domineering ways beside; and not a little of his looks. In him you would have seen a man of some size. Four hundred pounds he weighed."

Astrid opened her eyes at this, and Gunnar's jaw dropped in amazement. An enormous person this Johan Printz must have been indeed. It was hard to conceive of it.

Lars nodded. "Yes, four hundred pounds, no less, it was said. The Indians called him *The Big Tub*. And how he could drink! Still he was a good governor even if he was strict and hard. He did much for our colony. Half a dozen log forts rose in almost no time. He built a grand house for himself on Tinicum Island, together with a fort there. It was from Tinicum that he governed until he was called back to Sweden."

He paused, and Ingeborg contributed, "Then we had Juffrou Armgart's husband, Johan Papegoya, to take his place. But he disobeyed orders from Sweden and had to go there and give an account of himself. Governor Rising was sent to us next, but in a year the Dutch came and Swedish rule was altogether at an end."

"And now the Dutch have had to give in, and we must put up with the English," grumbled Gunnar.

"Come, come, my boy," Lars reproved him, "let us not complain too much, so long as we can keep our lands and make honest livings in peace. Governor Nicoll was a good and honorable governor, lenient, too, and saw justice done. Now that we have this Lovelace, let us remember that he may go back to England any day, and we may have a better man sent to take his place."

Gunnar shifted restlessly upon his three-legged stool. "If no one speaks out against injustice, it will never be put down."

"True," granted Lars, "but at present there is nothing that we Swedes can do to make things better. I advise you to be patient, to learn how to rule your temper, your tongue, your behavior. Above all, stay away from Evert Hindricksson, the Finn at Crane Hook. He is a desperate fellow and always in trouble. I would not have you follow his example."

"He is more settled now," protested Gunnar, "and

has become captain of a company of militia there. I wish I could join that company."

Lars raised a forbidding hand. "By no means. It would be to throw yourself head first into trouble. Stay away from Hindricksson."

At the mention of Evert Hindricksson anxious glances were exchanged between Astrid and her mother. They well remembered that Hindricksson had been banished from the settlement at Upland six years earlier, because he had twice attacked, and threatened the very life of Joran Kyn, a man of property there, a person extraordinarily good and gentle and excellent, as even Hindricksson had admitted. It would be disastrous in the extreme if Gunnar, hot-tempered and hasty as he was, should fall under the influence of a desperado like Hindricksson.

Lars rose from the table and went to get his pipe from the rack. "Remember, my boy," he said gravely to Gunnar, as he pressed the tobacco firmly into the bowl of the pipe with his thumb, "that you are to have nothing to do with Evert Hindricksson."

Gunnar made no response. A few minutes later he was romping gaily in the firelight with Karin and Kirsten, his grudges and resentments apparently forgotten. Yet Astrid knew how easy it would be to stir him to a rebellious mood again, and she quaked inwardly at the thought of the evil that might result to him if he should fall under the influence of Evert Hindricksson, or anyone like him.

CHAPTER III

ASTRID WAS PLUCKING spring flowers along the borders of the Bouwerie Wood. Spring sunshine touched to pale gold her flaxen braids and colored her fair skin to a deeper rose.

The giant oaks, of which the wood was composed, were in full leaf. Beneath the trees was spread a thick carpet of bloodroot, anemones, hepatica. One could not take a single step without crushing some of these.

Astrid had only to stoop and she could fill her hands at a sweep with the delicate blossoms, but she was selecting carefully the largest and loveliest.

These were not for herself. They were intended for a Dutch girl, Elsa Jens, whom she had made her friend. Elsa, slightly younger than herself, was an orphan, bound out from the Orphan House in New Castle to a hard-fisted Dutchman, Hans Brikker.

Two years earlier Brikker's overworked wife had died. It was then that he had applied to the Orphan House for a bound-girl to take care of his house. Elsa was not quite thirteen at that time, but he had thrust the entire work of the household upon her shoulders. She was sturdy, good natured, bore his meannesses and harsh treatment uncomplainingly, was industrious and neat.

Brikker gave her no leisure hours, permitted her no pleasures.

Happy in her own home, Astrid was moved to sympathy and pity at the sight of this young drudge who had no joys and no freedom. This had made Astrid reach out to Elsa in the beginning, made her smile upon the Dutch girl, made her bestow bright smiles and friendly words. Very soon, however, she gave her an affectionate friendship that was the sole comfort of Elsa's hard life.

Today, as soon as Astrid had gathered a large and handsome bunch of flowers, she would carry it to Elsa and hand it to her over the half-door of Hans Brikker's dwelling while he was absent in his field or upon other business. It would give Elsa a taste of woodland springtime.

In the midst of her pleasant task Astrid was imagining how Elsa would beam at sight of the flowers, how she would clasp them in her stubby fingers, how she would bury her broad face in the petals to inhale the faint fragrance.

A road skirted the wood. This opened at the northeast end of the village, bent sharply away to the right across the bridge over the Broad Dyke, and thence went straight on to Finland, Upland, and Tinicum. It was called the Tinicum Road and was the only road northward from New Castle in those days, and for long after.

Lars Nilsson's house, house lot, storehouse, bathhouse and barn were behind Astrid at a short distance to the left. His farmlands, fertile and well tended, stretched away beyond these buildings.

Clatter of hoofs upon the bridge across the Broad Dyke caught Astrid's attention. She raised herself, turned, and cupping one hand to shield her eyes from the brilliant sunshine, looked to the Broad Dyke to

She gathered a bunch of flowers to carry to Elsa

see who was approaching.

There was nothing to intercept her view for open fields lay on both sides of the road as it came out of the village. Hence she was able to see distinctly a woman riding toward her on a bay mare.

This woman sat her mare haughtily, and urged it forward at a smart pace. Arrogance showed in the lift of her head, in the curve of her determined mouth, in her small steely eyes, in the pointed arch of her pale eyebrows, in her dominant large nose and heavy jaws.

Dust powdered her plumed hat and the brown riding dress which covered her large frame. Her gloved hand gripped the reins firmly; it was evident that she would saw the bit without mercy if the mood seized her.

Astrid recognized her as Juffrou Armgart Printz Papegoya, the "proud lady of Tinicum," as the Swedes and Finns along the Delaware called her. Armgart Printz she called herself, dropping her married name Papegoya, and using the surname of her father, the notorious Johan Printz, once Governor of New Sweden on the Delaware.

Juffrou Armgart was as unpopular as her father had been, had the same domineering, irascible qualities which had finally lost him his governorship and sent him back to Sweden when the patient peaceful Swedes could no longer endure his tyranny.

His daughter had no power; the lack of it rankled in her, and made her more overbearing than ever. She resented bitterly this lack when Dutch rule usurped Swedish.

Nevertheless during Petrus Stuyvesant's governorship, and later when the British took all the region along the Delaware, she contrived to get back and to retain her father's possessions—the good farmlands at Printz Torp, and the island of Tinicum with its handsome mansion, its gardens and orchards.

In spite of these favors shown her by the alien governments, she considered that she had been allowed far less than her due.

Her lands were valuable, yet being what she was she had difficulty in obtaining anyone to work them for her. The mistress of Tinicum and Printz Torp drove hard bargains, gave small wages, and her demands were great. She needed men in her fields this very day. She had failed to get them and her thick brows were knit in an ugly frown.

This frown lifted slightly when she perceived Astrid standing near the road, the folds of her skirt stirring a little in the light breeze, the white sleeves and guimpe which her scarlet bodice confined dazzling in the spring sunshine. It was not the charming picture which Astrid made that caused Armgart Printz to rein in her mare sharply when she reached the girl. It was of herself and her own needs that she thought.

"Where is your father?" she demanded, sitting unbending in the saddle.

"He is plowing in his upper field, Juffrou. He will not be at home for several hours yet," replied Astrid with that respect which she had been taught to show to an exalted person however disagreeable.

Armgart's frown deepened for she wished to speak to Lars at once. "Tell him to come to me at Printz Torp early this evening," she said curtly. "I have work for him to do." She issued this as a command rather than a request. The girl's fair face flushed a little for she knew that Lars Nilsson would not have liked Juffrou Armgart's tone. Nevertheless she answered quietly, "I will give him your message, Juffrou."

Armgart struck the mare a smart blow with her silver-handled whip, dug in the spurs, and trotted off to Printz Torp in a cloud of dust.

Astrid paused for a moment to watch her disappearing, unaware that another traveler was approaching her by way of a wood trail striking in from the south and Mr. Augustine Hermann's cart track from Maryland, known as "The Old Man's Road."

This traveler was advancing toward her with the long swinging gait of the tireless walker. His dusty feet fell softly on the trail; his rough woolen knee-breeches, coarse hose, leathern jacket and shabby beaver hat were weather-stained, but he carried himself with audacity and an air of assurance.

Notwithstanding this, he had journeyed cautiously for reasons of his own through forests and meadows out of Maryland, had skirted the boundary of New Castle, and so had reached the continuing shelter of the Bouwerie Wood. His purpose in coming was known only to himself. He had not yet arrived at his journey's end, and was uncertain as to the quickest safest way of getting there. Perhaps this girl among the flowers could direct him.

Astrid was startled at hearing a man's voice, a voice that she did not know. She swung round quickly to discover whose it was. A tall stranger, the handsomest man she had ever seen, confronted her.

His dark hair hung thick under his beaver, his gray eyes were persuasive, his features were as perfect as features could be.

He was waiting for her answer, but she had not caught his words for he had spoken softly.

[35]

Her eyes sought his inquiringly, though without fear.

He repeated his question. "Which is the shortest way to Printz Torp, my good girl?"

"The road yonder, the Tinicum Road," she informed him, pointing it out, "leads straight to Printz Torp. If you keep to it you cannot go astray."

The stranger jerked his head in lieu of thanks.

"Printz Torp is a farm," Astrid added. "Juffrou Armgart Printz, the 'proud lady of Tinicum,' lives there."

"So I have heard," replied the stranger.

He, too, vanished.

"It may be," thought Astrid, "that he seeks work. In that case the mistress of Printz Torp will be glad to see him." With that she dismissed him from her mind. He seemed to her no more than a harmless traveler inquiring his way among unfamiliar surroundings.

Before she carried the flowers she had gathered to Elsa, she went to her father in the upper field and delivered Armgart Printz's message.

Lars Nilsson leaned a moment on his plow handles. His calm face remained impassive, though his accents in replying were decisive.

"Whenever the mistress of Tinicum wishes to speak with me, she must do it in my house or in my own fields. I am not her servant that I should be obliged to wait upon her at Printz Torp when she chooses to demand it."

CHAPTER IV

ELSA SAT ON THE DOOR-
step of Hans Brikker's house patching an old pair of
his woolen breeches.

Her round face, under the blue calico cap that
covered her head and hid all of her hair except two
tight braids which dangled down her back, was tired
and discouraged. She had worked hard throughout
the morning ever since peep of day. Yet she had
scarcely cleared away the dishes after the midday

meal and put the kitchen to rights, when Brikker had flung the torn breeches at her, bidding her peremptorily to make a good job of their repair.

Seldom did Elsa lose heart altogether, but she had been longing for days to slip off to the Bouwerie Wood for a few minutes to have at least a glimpse of the spring flowers. From the beginning there had not been the slightest hope of such a joy. Because there was no hope, tears dropped from her dark gray eyes onto the faded stuff in her lap while she set the huge patches and drove her needle through the tough cloth.

Brikker was away, looking after his cattle, and so Elsa dared to weep.

The upper half of the house door was open and showed the spotless Dutch kitchen, the fire, the dark settles and chests, the fresh window curtains, the ruffled pawn that decked the mantel-shelf.

To keep all these in the approved Dutch manner took every particle of Elsa's time and girlish strength.

Astrid's voice made her lift her tear-stained face in surprise, for she had not known that her friend was near. She saw the flowers in Astrid's hands, and a change, swift as that in an April sky, swept over her countenance, drying her tears and bringing a sunny smile.

"Oh!" she cried, and then her breath stopped for an instant at the sight of so much beauty.

"For you," said Astrid, dropping the flowers into Elsa's lap and taking a seat beside her on the doorstep, her back against the lower half door.

Elsa clasped the blossoms, buried her face in them as Astrid had guessed that she would, exclaimed over them ecstatically, and held them to her breast. Patches, grief, weariness were quite forgotten.

"They must not be allowed to wither," she said presently, "but I must hide them where my master won't see them. He would take them from me and throw them into the fire, for he can't bear to let me have a pleasure."

"Put them into water now and hide them," advised Astrid, rising to go home after they had talked for a little while. "I must not stay any longer for if Hans Brikker came and found me here, he might scold you after I was gone."

Elsa heaved a sigh. She found it difficult to part from Astrid so soon.

Astrid kissed her affectionately as she took leave. "You must not get a single cross word on my account. He gives you far too many as it is."

Hans Brikker's house stood in the village on Mink Street, a short distance from the upper part of the

Market Plaine. Astrid had gone but a short distance from it when she heard Elsa's voice raised in a piercing shriek, followed by silence.

Alarmed, and believing that Elsa was alone and that some dreadful accident had befallen her, Astrid flew back to the house to give help.

One piercing shriek she had heard and then no more, but as Astrid ran faster, drew nearer, she heard smothered choking sobs and pitiful gasps as if from unendurable pain.

What could have happened, oh, what could have happened in those few minutes since she left her friend? Astrid wondered, sick at heart.

Her question was answered quickly when she reached the house and directed her anxious gaze over the open half door into the kitchen.

Elsa was on her knees upon the floor, cowering under a rain of cutting blows from a stout birch rod wielded mercilessly by Hans Brikker.

Furious anger added itself to the horror that Astrid felt. Like a tornado she swept into the kitchen, seized the birch rod by the middle before it could fall again upon its quivering victim.

"Run, Elsa, run!" she cried, clinging with might and main to the rod which Brikker would inevitably succeed in wresting from her. "Run, run!" she cried again, swaying this way and that like a reed as Brik-ker, white with rage, strove to shake her hold from the birch rod.

Elsa stumbled to her feet. Enormous welts from

the cruel strokes of the rod were upon her back. Streaks of blood stained her dress and sleeves. Her eyes were red from weeping. She trembled violently from head to foot.

Yet she never would run to safety (if there were safety for her anywhere) while Astrid fought for her single-handed.

By a powerful wrench Brikker freed the rod from Astrid's clinging hands, swung it on high and shook it. "Get out of my house, you meddling Swedish wench," he roared, "unless you want to feel this rod yourself. What I do in my house to my servant is my own business, not yours."

He turned on Elsa. "Down on your knees again, you lazy slut. I'll teach you to waste your time with flowers when I give you breeches to mend."

On the floor, his cowhide boot set upon them, were the spring blossoms, crushed almost to a pulp. He had caught Elsa in the act of putting them in water and before she had had time to hide them.

Astrid's voice rang out. "No, Elsa, you shall not kneel. You shall not take another blow. Run to the Orphan House, fast, fast, and let them see how you have been beaten. Don't be afraid for me. Hans Brikker will not dare to strike me. I will accuse him before the magistrate if he tries it."

"So, you dare me in my own house," bawled the Dutchman, losing all control over himself. "I will teach you something, too."

Even in his fury he realized that he must not venture to strike with the rod. But there were other ways of wreaking vengeance upon her for her interference.

He would shake her till her teeth rattled.

[43]

He threw down the rod and advanced upon her, his fingers working as though he could hardly wait to clutch her.

In a flash Astrid was out of his reach. Swift as lightning she snatched up the birch rod and flung it into the fire. The birch caught all along its oily bark and spouted flame.

Determined to catch her, to corner her, to shake her as a cat shakes a mouse, Brikker pursued her, preventing her by his bulk from slipping past him to the door.

Astrid was light as a feather on her feet, agile, swift. Hans Brikker was clumsy in his movements but he was doggedly persistent.

Again and again and again he almost seized her, again and again he blocked her way. Again and yet again her swiftness saved her.

Elsa had vanished. Not to go to the Orphan House as Astrid had bidden her, but to summon help for her friend, to bring someone who could prevent harm to her.

She had hurried into the street as fast as her shaking limbs could carry her. Now she was looking distractedly to right and left, hoping to catch a passer-by sooner than she could fetch a neighbor. Gerritt Jansen the smith was strong but Astrid might be badly

She flew back to the house to give help

harmed before he could be brought to the rescue. Men were not apt to be in their homes at this hour of the day. Elsa was sure that women would be of no use in this case.

She was about to rush to the smithy, though it was not close by, when all at once she saw a young and stalwart gentleman entering Mink Street from the Market Plaine. No one else was in sight.

Elsa flew to him. "Sir, come, oh, come quickly and stop Hans Brikker," she begged piteously. She stood directly in front of the young man, barring his progress.

Checked thus unexpectedly, he surveyed the girl with frank astonishment. Her swollen eyes and tear-stained cheeks roused his compassion.

"Stop Hans Brikker?" he echoed. "From what?"

"He is trying to hurt Astrid Nilsson, my friend. Come, come," she insisted, tugging at his sleeve.

Philip Stanton required no further urging. The girl before him was in distress. A girl whom he could not see was in danger. That was sufficient to make him follow Elsa's guidance.

In a couple of dozen long strides he was at Hans Brikker's open door. One stride more took him over the sill. In another minute he had Hans Brikker by the collar.

On the way to the house Elsa had told Stanton briefly in sobbing breaths what Brikker had done. It filled him with burning indignation.

All at once Brikker felt himself being dragged vigorously backward.

"Coward, brute!" Stanton thundered in his ears. "You have beaten your poor bound-girl cruelly, and the Orphan Master shall know of it and protect her in future. Touch but a hair of this other maid's head, and Captain Carr himself shall hear of it from me."

Stanton emphasized his words by a tightening of his strong hand on the Dutchman's neckband.

Half choked, Brikker sputtered, "Then let her stay away from my house, the good-for-nothing Swede. Coming here, making my bound-girl lazy, putting notions into her head, trying to stop me from giving my servant a beating when she deserves it. And who are you," he bellowed, "walking in here and meddling with my business?"

By a powerful effort he contrived to break from Stanton's grasp, and wheeled on him like an angry bull. He shook his fist in Stanton's face. "Get out of my house, get out of my house," he yelled. "Do I have to throw you out? Threatening me with Captain Carr, is it?"

Stanton surveyed him up and down coolly. "With

Captain Carr. Yes. Captain Carr happens to be my father's oldest friend. He knows me well and will believe me when I tell him how you have been bullying helpless maids. He will put a stop to it. Be sure of that."

Brikker began to wilt. Captain Carr stood at the head of authority in New Castle, representing Governor Sir Francis Lovelace who was in New York. He could make matters go very hard for anyone if he chose. Moreover, the Dutchman had secret reasons for wanting to keep on the good side of Captain Carr.

Astrid, standing quiet by the hearth, Elsa's hand clasped in hers, perceived the effect of Stanton's threat upon Brikker and how a sickly pallor overspread his fat cheeks and pendulous jowl.

"If my servant does her work," he mumbled, "she will have no cause to complain, nor will anybody else if they tend to their own business." His small mean eyes roved from side to side, meeting none of those leveled upon him.

"Elsa, come with me," said Astrid. "I will go with you to the Orphan House. The Orphan Master must know how dreadfully you have been treated, must see for himself. I will tell him what I myself saw."

"Take my servant from me," howled Brikker.

"No, that I will not allow." He was too well aware of Elsa's value to give her up without a struggle.

"She will go at once," decreed Stanton firmly. "And I shall go with the maids and see that justice is done. Follow us if you like."

Follow he did, trudging sullenly in the wake of Philip Stanton, scowling at the back of the young man's fine green broadcloth coat with voluminous tails and wide pockets, his handsome beaver hat with drooping green plume held in place by a jeweled ornament; scowling at the backs of Elsa and Astrid.

The two girls walked beside Stanton.

"You were barely in time, sir," Astrid murmured gratefully. "A minute more and he would have caught me."

"I would have had him jailed for certain if he had harmed you," replied Stanton, his hazel eyes regarding her kindly and then traveling on to Elsa. "We shall make sure that he gives this poor maid no more beatings."

"Oh, sir," was all that Elsa could utter out of her full heart.

Their voices were pitched too low for Brikker to hear what was said. He had no need to strain his ears when the four arrived at the Orphan House.

Philip Stanton set the case forth in plain round

terms. Astrid told her story. Elsa was questioned on all points. She was taken to an inner room, where the matron in charge had her pull off her dress and show her back. A mass of great welts, broken skin, bleeding flesh, bruises were found upon it.

"Poor child, poor child!" exclaimed the matron, throwing up her hands, horrified at the sight. "This must never be allowed to happen again."

She presented her report to the Orphan Master, casting indignant glances at Brikker as she spoke.

There could be no doubt as to Brikker's guilt, nor did he attempt to deny that he had given Elsa a beating, declaring that she fully deserved it and that he had a right to give it.

The Orphan Master reproved him sternly. "Learn once for all, Hans Brikker, that you have no such right. If you do not know how to behave yourself as a good master, this girl shall be taken from you and bound out to a better one. I allow you one more trial, and only one. See to it, in particular, that there are no more beatings. We know Elsa, and that she is a good, industrious, neat girl. She shall stay here and be taken care of until her back is healed. Then she will go to you again for as long as you treat her decently. You will now pay us a fine of thirty guilders for what you did to her today."

Brikker ground his teeth as he laid down the money.

Philip Stanton bestowed on him a final warning. "Remember what I mentioned to you about Captain Carr."

He received a resentful glare from Brikker in reply.

Astrid was comforted to know that Elsa was to have a few days of care in the Orphan House, but above all that she was to receive no more beatings.

"You were a brave maid," Stanton commended. He was walking a short distance with her after they had said good-by to Elsa and left her in the matron's hands.

Astrid drooped her head. "Not very," she confessed. "I could not see Elsa treated as she was. Anger and pity made me bold then. But when Hans Brikker tried to catch me, chased me round and round, and I could not get to the door, I was afraid then—terribly afraid."

Stanton smiled. "It took courage just the same," he contested. "Your parents will not let you enter that fellow's house again."

"My parents will not forbid me, for Elsa's sake, to go to the door at least and speak to her, though I shall not step inside."

"But when they hear what has happened to you?" he asked.

"I have suffered no harm," she answered. "I shall tell them what has been done to poor Elsa, but not what Hans Brikker tried to do to me. It would make my father too angry. Trouble would come of it."

"Be wise, then, when you go to speak to Elsa," Stanton advised her, "wise, and very careful."

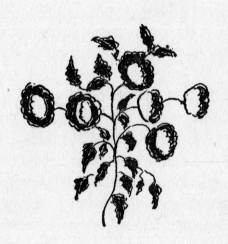

CHAPTER V

LARS NILSSON DID NOT GO to Armgart Printz, and unexpectedly, the "proud lady of Tinicum" had a very different visitor, and found herself engaged with quite other matters that evening than the problem of how to get her fields tilled.

At the hour of dusk the tall stranger who had inquired his way of Astrid presented himself at Juffrou

Armgart's door and asked speech with the mistress at Printz Torp.

The Finnish serving-woman who had answered his knock squinted at him curiously out of her shrewd little pale blue eyes set deep in her wrinkled face. She could see for herself that he was either Swede or Finn, but since he was a stranger in these parts, she wondered what his business could be with her mistress.

"Your name?" she asked, for she knew better than to usher anyone in to the "proud lady of Tinicum" without her express permission, especially a stranger whom she did not know.

"My name can wait," returned the man curtly. "Tell her that a messenger from Sweden is here."

Olga Stark bowed hastily. The man did not look to her like a gentleman, but there was a hint of command in his voice and bearing and she took it for granted that he must have come from Armgart's husband who was now in Sweden. If this were the case, she must not fail in proper respect to him. Notwithstanding, she requested him to wait in the hall while she went to give Armgart Printz his message.

Left alone, the stranger brushed a fleck or two of dust from his breeches, settled his collar neatly, smoothed his hose and his hair. Most of the dust of travel he had removed before he approached the house. He wished to make as good an impression as possible when he was brought face to face with the mistress of Printz Torp.

Olga's wooden shoes clattering toward him gave notice that she was returning. He straightened himself to his towering height and waited for Armgart's answer.

"The mistress will see you," said Olga, and led him a little distance down the passage which was bare except for a massive oaken chest or two set against the wall.

Armgart received the stranger in her great room. She sat stiffly in her broad high-backed chair as though it were a throne and she herself a sovereign. Her gaze, cold and searching, surveyed the man appraisingly as he bowed before her. She did not incline her own head in the slightest.

"Your name," she demanded imperiously, "and your business?"

Her scrutiny of him had been brief, but it had not escaped her that he was markedly taller and handsomer than any man that she had seen in the colony hitherto.

"My name is Königsmarck," he told her, "and my business is of the utmost importance and secrecy."

Armgart's brows rose in surprise. The name of Königsmarck was well known and of great distinction in Sweden. She had supposed that she knew every member of that noted family. Yet this man was an utter stranger to her. How was he related to them, if at all?

She regarded him keenly and with distrust.

He perceived it, and went on without giving her a chance to voice it.

"My name is Königsmarck," he repeated distinctly. "I am the son of General Count Königsmarck by an early and obscure marriage. My mother is long since dead. For private reasons my father has never publicly acknowledged me, but I am in his favor, nevertheless, and in that of other exalted persons. If I succeed in what I have been sent to do, it will be so much to the advantage of the King of Sweden that all who join with me in the attempt will profit richly by it, and I shall be openly acknowledged by my father as his eldest son."

Juffrou Armgart was only partially convinced, but she was curious to learn the nature of this secret business. She assumed an air of haughty condescension and, shifting her heavy gold wedding ring carelessly round and round upon her thumb, she said indifferently, "Whoever you may be, you are at liberty to speak and state your errand."

The man took the chair which she indicated. It was a chair of considerable size but his large and powerful frame filled it. He fixed upon her the unwavering gaze of his steel gray eyes, and began to speak in audible yet guarded tones.

"We shall not be interrupted or overheard?" he inquired, before going further.

"No one ventures to interrupt me when I am busy," returned Armgart coldly, her ringed fingers clasped in her lap.

"Nor to listen without being seen?" persisted he with a sardonic smile.

"None would dare," she snapped.

Königsmarck, as he called himself, proceeded.

It was a bold scheme and a venturesome that he laid before her; nothing less than to foment an uprising of the Swedes and Finns along the Delaware, to wrest authority from the English and regain the territory for Sweden.

Armgart's lip curled contemptuously. "They can never be persuaded to it. They are like oxen, these Swedes, these Finns that we have hereabouts. They let themselves be goaded and driven. They will put up with anything for the sake of peace, and to be allowed to keep their properties. First they let the

Dutchman, Petrus Stuyvesant, conquer them and settle his Dutch among us. They plundered us well. Next they submitted to the English. Now this Lovelace lords it over them, makes his own laws, changes them when it suits him, upsets the course of justice. Bah! They let themselves be driven like oxen, like sheep, these stupid Swedes and Finns. No one can stir them to rise up against him."

Her anger mounted as she poured this out. She thumped the chair arm with her thick fist, her cheeks flushed scarlet, her pig's eyes blazing.

"I will rouse them," asserted Königsmarck, his square jaws set.

Juffrou Armgart laughed in his face. "You think well of yourself."

"With reason," retorted Königsmarck composedly.

"Perhaps you have some grudge of your own that you wish to pay off," she suggested disagreeably.

"We all have grudges, you among the rest. We can pay off our grudges together. It is best that we unite our efforts."

"Do you think for an instant that I will ruin myself? Stick my head into a noose, as it were?" scoffed Armgart.

"So far as you are concerned, you need run into

no danger," he said. "None but I and those above me need know that you are in any way linked with the attempt. That shall be as you choose, but it will be of assistance in the carrying out of the scheme to have your suggestions from time to time. Besides that, you are acquainted with the people in these settlements, and can advise me, who am a stranger, as to which of the men, Swedes or Finns, it will be safe for me to approach; a few men who are brave and discreet, who can keep secrets, who will stand up for their rights. It is essential to me to know this. That is why I have come to you."

Armgart considered. There was power in the man's face, strikingly revealed by the flickering candlelight. She recognized it, this daughter of the enormous domineering old Governor Johan Printz. Her pride was flattered that Königsmarck had sought her out before he went elsewhere.

"The man has some sense," she told herself. "He knows the right person to ask, the person who should have the first word to say in this matter, myself."

"Very well," she said aloud. "Provided that you swear to keep it a profound secret that I have anything whatsoever to do with this venture, I will advise. Remember, I take no risks, now, nor in the future."

Königsmarck inclined his head to hide the gleam of triumph in his eyes. "I swear it," he said.

Armgart was satisfied. "Listen carefully then. These are the men who will be most likely to join with you, who will be of the most service. Go first to Hindrich Collmann, a Swede. He is an honorable man and one who hates injustice. He has property and influence. He would be running no risk except to himself, for he has no family, not even a wife. If you can persuade him, you have gained much. He knows the Indian language well and the Indians are always ready to assist him in whatever he wishes to do. Moreover, they have always been friendly to the Swedes."

"I will seek him first of all," assented Königsmarck.

"Next, there is Evert Hindricksson, a Finn. He loves to fight and was in trouble more than once while he was a laborer in Upland. The people at Upland drove him away from there. Now he is settled at Crane Hook and has been made a captain of militia in that place. He may be of great use to you, as you can readily understand."

"His help should be of the greatest value," agreed Königsmarck.

"Do not overlook Jan Stalcop, Juns Junstersen,

Olle Fransen. Those are men of means." She tipped them off on her fingers as she mentioned them, her eyes half shut, her sandy brows knit.

"Of course there are others," she continued. "Lars Nilsson and his son Gunnar, Eric Helm, too. He is young, like Gunnar, but young blood will be needed, especially if it comes to fighting. Hindricksson knows them all and where they are to be found. So does Hindrich Collmann."

Königsmarck remained seated, expecting her to go on. Instead, she waved her hand authoritatively to show that the interview was ended. "I have told you enough for the present," she said.

Königsmarck rose and thanked her. He had gained more than he had hoped for in this first meeting. "You will permit me to consult you again sometime, gracious lady?" he asked.

"On the express understanding that I am to be involved in no risks," replied Armgart crisply.

"In no risks," repeated Königsmarck, bowing himself to the door.

The "proud lady of Tinicum" remained in her chair. She heard his footsteps retreating along the passage, heard the house door close after him. From her place her eyes traveled absently about the room, over the wooden mugs painted in bright colors, over the plates and dishes ranged close together on high shelves along the walls a little below the beamed ceiling, over the brilliantly embroidered scarfs of Swedish workmanship which hung like banners below the shelves, over the fire-sticks (wooden splints) stuck in stout iron holders attached to the walls, over the curtained bed built into the corner, over the tall floor-clock, the hooded fireplace, the clothes rail suspended near the door.

She looked at them absently while she weighed circumspectly the dangers of the scheme which Königsmarck had laid before her, the risks to herself if she allowed herself to embark in it.

Her eyes grew cunning and her lips set themselves in a straight line. She sat bolt upright, her large head held arrogantly on her thick neck and massive shoulders.

"I shall run no risks whatever, shall do nothing that will betray me," she promised herself. "No proof shall ever be found against me that I have taken any mischievous part in this most dangerous venture."

CHAPTER VI

A COUPLE OF WEEKS later Astrid was crossing the Market Plaine, the tree-shaded green in the center of the town laid out by Petrus Stuyvesant in 1655.

An empty basket hung on her arm. It had been filled with fresh eggs and a pat of butter, but she had sold these to steady customers and the money she had received for them was safely deposited in the cloth pocket which hung from her waist.

On the green she encountered Eric Helm. He turned about and walked beside her. There was something which he felt she ought to know, although perhaps she had heard it already.

"A stranger has come to these parts, Astrid," he began, suiting his step to hers.

Astrid glanced up at him quickly.

"A man who says his name is Königsmarck, and that he is Swedish, but the folk hereabout call him the Long Finn. He is uncommonly tall and by no means bad looking, but he is here to make trouble."

"Perhaps it was he who asked me the way to Printz Torp one day," interposed Astrid, and told him what she remembered about the stranger.

"The very same person," pronounced Eric with conviction. "He is talking to Swedes and Finns wherever he can find any who are willing to listen, telling them how unjustly they are being treated, trying to stir them to demand their rights. He gets these men together secretly and makes fiery speeches. Have not your father or Gunnar mentioned him?"

"No," returned Astrid, "but if father knows of him, he surely will not listen to him. My father is always for peace."

"Gunnar?" inquired Eric, regarding her steadily. It was Gunnar who concerned him most.

"Gunnar," replied Astrid slowly, and her cheek paled. "Oh, I hope Gunnar will not pay any heed to him," she said, stroking her apron nervously. "He would be a dangerous man for Gunnar."

"He is," responded Eric. "The man can persuade, speaks strongly, knows how to rouse the feelings."

"He has spoken to you?"

"Yes, at the very outset. But I gave him to understand at once that I would not join in any uprising, nor go to his secret meetings. My father said the same to him. He has not tried us again."

"Gunnar has not mentioned the man to my parents," Astrid declared positively. "Nor to me," she added.

"If only the fellow had not come," deplored Eric. "He will assuredly make matters worse than they are already. Those who join with him will be ruined."

Astrid walked beside him in a dead silence. Fear for Gunnar overcame her.

Eric realized the effect his words and the situation itself were having upon her. He made haste to offer what reassurance he could. "Listen, Astrid. Gunnar is open of heart and speech. If he has seen and heard Long Finn, he will not be able to keep it to himself.

Whether he means to or not, he will blurt it out; to me, if to no one else. Count upon it. On my part, I will spare no arguments to make him see the folly of going along with Long Finn in such schemes."

On the strength of this, Astrid compelled herself to hope for the best. She resolved not to approach the subject with Gunnar unless she had more cause than she had at present.

Her alarm was increased, however, before many days had passed. She was busy one evening in the flower garden which she and her mother had planted in the space between the log house and the fence which surrounded the house lot. The law of New Castle required that house lots in the town should be fenced in.

This small plot of fragrance and beauty was mainly under Astrid's care. She delighted in keeping it free from weeds, in training its vines, in trimming its borders. Karin and Kirsten were free to pluck the flowers on certain designated plants. They must not meddle with the rest.

Astrid dearly loved the quiet hour after supper which was entirely her own, in which she could attend to the garden beds, as she was doing this evening.

The day had been hot, but with the approach of

night the air had grown cooler and a breeze had sprung up.

Lars, in his shirt sleeves, was puffing away at his pipe on a long bench outside the house door. Ingeborg sat by him, knitting rapidly upon a pair of hose for Gunnar. He was hard on his stockings, and ground enormous holes in them.

Karin and Kirsten were patting the earth around their special plants, pretending to be skilled gardeners.

Directly supper was over, Gunnar had strolled toward the Bouwerie Wood. No one had paid any attention to that for he had been in the habit of doing it ever since he was a child.

Lars had glanced after him as he went, and had remarked to Ingeborg, "Perhaps I have succeeded in getting a little sense into that fellow's head at last. He has not grumbled near so much lately about how affairs are run in the town and elsewhere."

His wife had smiled contentedly over her knitting. "I hope you are right, Lars," she murmured.

Astrid bent a trifle lower to the spicy pinks in the border. She had heard what they said, but doubted her father's success. Though Gunnar had grumbled less, she had caught an odd expression on his face on various occasions when he supposed himself to be unobserved. It suggested to her that he was keeping something to himself, something that he was not willing to speak of, or had been forbidden to divulge. To keep a secret was not natural to him.

Neither she nor her parents imagined when they saw Hindrich Collmann entering the gate this evening as dusk began to fall, that his coming was in any way connected with Gunnar.

Hindrich Collmann was a highly respected man in New Castle. Though he was a lover of justice and good government, he had always been a peaceful person, never engaged in brawls nor in conflict with the authorities.

Lars and Ingeborg took it for granted that he had come, as usual, on a purely neighborly visit. They were taken completely by surprise, therefore, when after greetings had been interchanged and he had accepted the seat offered him on the bench, he began to speak of something quite different from crops and the weather.

"Well, Lars," he said, "it looks as though we Swedes are to regain control of our settlements along this river, that we shall have a New Sweden once more." Collmann uttered this with an air of confidence and satisfaction.

Lars jerked his pipe from his mouth and shot Collmann a glance of startled inquiry. "What do you mean by that?" he ejaculated.

The swift movement of Ingeborg's knitting needles ceased abruptly, while she, too, waited for Collmann to explain himself.

Astrid alone knew what he meant. Instantly her thoughts flew to Gunnar. She stepped nearer, listening intently.

Karin and Kirsten kept on with their innocent play.

"A man has come among us—surely you must have heard of him by this time—who has been sent by the King of Sweden with instructions to band us together, to accept this man as our leader, to throw off the yoke of the English and become Swedish subjects again."

Astrid caught her breath. *To throw off the yoke of the English altogether!* That would be a tremendous undertaking!

Lars regarded Collmann incredulously. "Who is this man?" he demanded. "He must be out of his senses. I have heard nothing of him nor of his crazy ideas until this instant. Nor has my wife."

Ingeborg made haste to corroborate this. "Not a single word of the sort has reached my ears, but then, you know, I seldom hear the neighbors' gossip." She fell to knitting briskly again.

"Gunnar has heard," thought Astrid. "That accounts for his odd looks. Yet he has not mentioned this stranger to us. He should have done so; he should have done so." It was because he knew his father would have no sympathy with any such uprising, nor be inclined to take the word of an utter stranger, that Gunnar had forced himself to be silent.

Astrid drew still nearer so that she might not lose a word of what Hindrich Collmann was saying, nor of her father's replies.

"The stranger tells us that his name is Königs-marck, that he is the son of the great Königsmarck in Sweden. From Sweden, therefore, he comes. We call him the Long Finn. He is the tallest, handsomest man ever seen in these colonies."

"And you believe these claims on the bare word of a perfect stranger? You astonish me, Hindrich Collmann."

Collmann flushed a little, but he smiled amiably and held his ground. "Ah, but you should see him, Lars, should hear him. You yourself would be convinced."

"By no means," asserted Lars emphatically, drawing strongly on his pipe.

"Why not? No less a person than Juffrou Armgart

Printz believes there may be something in his claims," insisted Collmann.

Lars gave his characteristic shrug of his shoulders. "Juffrou Armgart may credit what she pleases. That does not concern me. Let her get into mischief if she chooses. For my part, I intend to keep myself and my family out of it."

"Stop, Lars. Do not say that. Surely you should be willing to take part in any effort that puts an end to injustice and that will better the condition of our people."

Lars answered promptly. "No one dislikes injustice more than I do. But have sense, Collmann. Here we are, a few Swedes and Finns scattered along the river from Tinicum Island to Fort Casimir. In New Castle itself we are not many. What would we be able to do against English soldiers who can be brought against us in great numbers, to shoot us down, or march us off to prison and be kept there for God alone knows how long?"

Astrid shuddered at such a prospect for those who might follow the Long Finn.

Ingeborg sighed sharply. Before Collmann could interpose, Lars went on.

"I am not always satisfied with the doings of this Governor Lovelace who has authority over us at present, but I should be far less satisfied if I were put in prison for rebellion, with my farm taken from me and my family left to bear as best they could the consequences of my folly. You have no family, Collmann, only yourself to risk."

"Königsmarck assures us that when we are ready to rise, the King of Sweden will have two ships of war outside the Capes, loaded with soldiers who will reinforce us in strength. That will give us the upper hand and bring success."

Lars threw back his head and laughed aloud. "Let him who will believe that. There will be no warships from Sweden, no victory. The man is an impostor. Moreover, I gave my word to obey English laws and my word is good. Besides that, Sweden gave us no help when the Dutch took our settlements, nor when the English did the same. This is a new land, our homes and our life are here, and we must live in it as peaceably as we can with our neighbors. Say no more to me, Collmann. You will never persuade me to such folly as you speak of. No, nor any of mine."

Hindrich Collmann stirred on the long bench and opened his lips as though he were about to contradict him. He thought better of it, however, and contented himself with saying, "That is a matter which each of us must decide for himself, Lars." And having been rebuffed so decidedly on what he had come about, he turned the talk to affairs which had nothing to do with Long Finn.

Astrid continued to ponder what he had said previously. Her mother's voice broke in upon her. "Fetch in the children, Astrid. They should be in bed."

Astrid obeyed, but while she was making the twins ready for the night, answering their sleepy questions, tucking them up in the wall bed after their brief prayer was said, her mind was not with them. Then and after Hindrich Collmann was gone, she was wondering whether Gunnar was walking in the Bouwerie Wood, or whether he was with the Long Finn, drinking in his seditious arguments.

Lars had fastened the shutters and was preparing to drop the bar across the house door when Gunnar came home.

His father bent upon him a searching look. "You stay late in the Bouwerie Wood, Gunnar," he observed. "A little longer and I should have had to fasten the door upon you. We keep early hours here, as you know. Astrid and your mother are already in bed."

"I had not meant to stay so long," apologized Gunnar sheepishly.

From her pillow Astrid heard her father speaking gravely. She peeped out through an opening in the bed curtains, and saw him lay an admonishing hand on Gunnar's shoulder.

"Be careful, my son, that you do not mix yourself up with this stranger, the Long Finn, of whom Hindrich Collmann has been telling me this evening. Only harm can come of it."

Astrid marked how Gunnar gazed steadily into his father's eyes for an instant, then dropped his head, and without a word climbed the log ladder to his bed in the loft.

She pulled the bed curtains close and buried her face in her pillow, oppressed by forebodings which she could not shake off.

CHAPTER VII

THE HEAVY THWACKING of the reed (or sley), which forced each thread of weft snugly to its place in the warp threads set in the loom, ceased. The loom stood in the loft of Lars Nilsson's storehouse.

Astrid stepped down from her seat on the narrow weaver's bench in front of the loom. She had been weaving diligently throughout the hot summer afternoon and she was glad that she need do no more today. While at work, she had viewed with satisfaction the evenness and firmness of the woolen cloth growing beneath her skillful fingers. Her mother would be as pleased with it as she was herself.

Every inch of cloth used for the garments of the family was the product of the spinning and weaving by Astrid or her mother.

The girl's white forehead, bordered by her embroidered cap, was damp with perspiration. She wiped it dry with a corner of her striped apron and went to the open window for a breath of outside air before she descended from the loft.

This window afforded her a favorite outlook toward the little town, scarcely more than a village, toward Fort Casimir and away to the Delaware River, silvery in the late afternoon light.

A boat was putting out from the New Castle shore. She guessed rightly that Eric Helm was in it with bait and nets. Her eyes rested on it for a few minutes, watching its course.

Then her vision swept the nearer landscape. She noted a faint curl of smoke rising from the chimney of the house belonging to the surly Dutchman, Hans Brikker. The house was hidden by the trees. Astrid thought of her friend, Elsa Jens, drudging there as usual from dawn to dark.

Fortunately for Elsa, her sturdy frame did not sink under her burdens. Her chief comfort still was Astrid's friendship, though opportunities of enjoying her companionship had become rarer than ever. Yet she never forgot that she had Astrid's affection and understanding, and that helped greatly; nor did she ever forget how Astrid had saved her from Hans Brikker's rod.

Astrid contrived to come to her now and again when Brikker was away from the house. A tap on the half door or on the shutter would bring Elsa beaming to the opening to exchange a dozen words or so, to receive Astrid's smile, and feel Astrid's friendly arm around her shoulders.

Some days had passed since the two girls had met.

"I must manage to see Elsa tomorrow," Astrid thought, turning from the window. She went to the stairway, merely a huge log with notches hewn in it along its entire length to serve as steps. It was placed on a slant, one end fastened to a square opening in the floor of the loft, the other secured to the planks of the floor below.

The loft, furnished with loom, small flax wheel, big wool wheel, two rudely built box beds filled with straw and used for guests when needed, had been bright enough for Astrid while she was at work.

Now, as she lowered herself notch by notch down the stair, the loft and the objects in it were beginning to grow dim as the afternoon waned.

She did not have to wait until the following day to have speech with Elsa. She was driving the red cow home for the evening milking, when a familiar figure hurried to her across the pasture—Elsa, out of breath, braids flying, calico cap awry.

"Astrid," she panted, seizing her friend by the arm, "tell your father that Hans Brikker intends to steal his unmarked pigs—every one."

"Stop, Elsa, get your breath," Astrid bade her. "You have run too fast."

"I had to. Hans saw your father and Gunnar penning those pigs. Afterward I heard him mumbling to himself, as he does sometimes when he thinks he is alone, mumbling and chuckling spitefully, 'I'll mark that Swede's pigs, but with my mark, Hans Brikker's mark, and I'll not be slow about it either.'"

She stopped a second and then went on. "I was in the pantry, busy at the cheese press, and he thought I could not hear him. But I did, every word."

"How dare he put his mark on my father's pigs!" exclaimed Astrid hotly. "He can be taken to jail for doing that, and for stealing them. He would be well punished for it. Branded as a thief, perhaps, with the big T on his thumb."

"Oh, but I heard him mutter this, too," said Elsa, " 'Lars can do nothing to me for I have got leave from the magistrate to mark any pigs of mine that have been let run wild in the woods.' "

"Our pigs have been in our own woods," asserted Astrid. "The pen is there, too."

"Once the pigs are marked and taken away secretly, nothing can be proved against Hans," Elsa told her. "Get your father to be sure to mark them very early in the morning."

Astrid hastened her footsteps. "Be sure I will tell him. He will probably mark them all tonight."

She poked the red cow with a stick to drive her home faster.

Elsa hurried along beside her for a last word. "He need not do that, for Hans will be away at the tavern this evening with a friend. He never comes home till late. But early, early in the morning your father and Gunnar must get to the pen if they are to be in time."

"Thanks to you, Elsa; thanks to you," said Astrid gratefully. "My father owes you much."

Elsa threw out her hand in farewell, but turned her head to implore, "Above all things, do not let Hans Brikker find out that I have told you. He would beat me in spite of the Orphan Master—beat me black and blue."

"Trust us," cried Astrid after her.

Lars was smoking his pipe and resting on the settle when his daughter sped into the kitchen to give him Elsa's warning.

"That rascally Dutchman," he thundered, striking the arm of the settle with closed fist. "He thinks to steal my fine pigs, does he? If it were not that I want to catch him at it, I would mark them tonight. One mean thing after another he has done to me, but this would be the worst. If I can catch him at it, I'll have him put behind jail bars. That will teach him to leave me alone."

"Let me do the catching," said Gunnar from the other end of the settle. "You know you intended to start early tomorrow morning to mow the upper meadow. That, in itself, will be a long day's work for you. Hans Brikker will not be apt to have his musket with him, but I shall have mine. He knows I'm a good shot and I'll make him run."

"There should be two of us," affirmed Lars. "You could, of course, manage the business alone, but there must be a witness to what took place at the pen when Hans Brikker is brought before the magistrate. Other-wise there would only be your word against his, and the magistrate might credit his instead of yours."

"True enough," admitted Gunnar. "There must be two of us."

"I had meant to mark the pigs at my leisure," said Lars, wrinkling his brows in vexation. "I had supposed they would be perfectly safe in the pen, and at present we have good weather for haying. Well, we must do what we can. We will go together to mark the pigs instead, and be there before it is quite light."

He had no reason to think that anything would happen to interfere with this plan. The family ate supper; Lars smoked his pipe on the bench outside the door; Ingeborg sat knitting alongside him; Astrid weeded her garden. Gunnar went off to the pen in the woods, and came back to report that thus far no harm had been done.

No one noticed that Karin and Kirsten, chasing one another around the house, darted just once in and out of the storehouse which was forbidden ground to them. Rakes, saws, scythes, and various other implements used about the farm hung on its walls, or stood in its corners. That made it a place of danger for small children.

A large wooden rake, propped against the wall in a dusky corner, was accidentally knocked down by

Karin as she rushed after Kirsten on the way out. It fell between the log stair and the door but was hidden from sight by the dense shadows.

Shortly before bedtime a thunderstorm threatened.

Generally in summer, when the weather was good, the door and windows of the storehouse were left open day and night, but during storms they were closed tightly.

At the first thunderclap Lars rose from the bench, saying, "I must shut up the storehouse before the rain pours in."

The skies were inky black. Except when lightning flashed, the darkness was intense, outside the storehouse as well as within it.

But the storehouse was a place where order was accustomed to reign and Lars, familiar with every nook and corner of it, often boasted that in pitch dark he could lay his hand upon any object that he wanted in the little building.

He hastened to it tonight with confidence, going directly to the stair, intending to shut the upper windows first.

His foot caught in the rake which Karin had thrown down; he tripped, twisting his ankle violently in his effort to recover himself, and was thrown upon the lower steps of the stair.

Pain made him wince. To get to the upper floor and shut the windows there was impossible for him. Someone else must close the storehouse, for every least movement made him groan.

He managed by the help of the stair to pull himself upright. In the corner nearest him were several stout birch poles. He groped for and found one, and supporting himself by means of it, hobbled out of the door and to the house. Cold sweat broke out on his forehead with each step.

"Here is a mess, now," he grumbled to Ingeborg, when he had got to the settle and she was lowering his injured foot into a pail of hot water to ease his suffering. "I can neither go about my mowing tomorrow nor, what is more important, be with Gunnar at the pen. We shall have no witness to what goes on there."

"That you cannot help," replied his wife, bathing his foot with utmost tenderness.

Astrid looked up from the hearth, where she was settling securely upon a pile of red embers a pan filled with vinegar and salt to be heated and used in bandaging the foot when her mother removed it from the steaming water.

"Do not be troubled about a witness," she said. "I

will go with Gunnar, and shall see and hear everything that occurs. As for the hay, I can help there, too. Gunnar will mow and I will rake."

"That you should rake the hay is well enough," grunted Lars, who was suffering acutely, "but it would be a new idea to have a girl mixed up in such a business as this with Hans Brikker. There may be shooting. You might get hurt. No, Astrid, I shall not permit it."

Astrid took a long piece of old linen from the chest and began to tear it into strips for the bandage.

"Do not forbid me to go to the pen with Gunnar, father. It is important that there should be a witness. You have said so. I have good eyes, good ears, and if there is shooting, I shall have sense enough to keep out of the way of it." This said, she laid the strips of linen convenient to her mother's hand.

"Have it your own way then," consented Lars at last, unwillingly. "But mind that you keep well out of the way of the shooting."

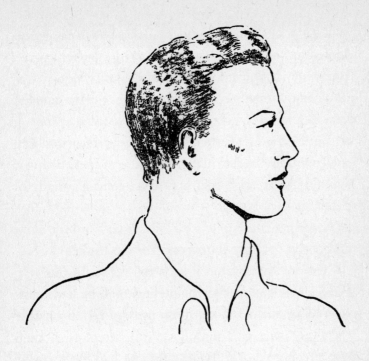

CHAPTER VIII

PALE LIGHT OF DAWN WAS
not yet showing in fields or meadows when Astrid
slipped through the darkness of her father's wood
with Gunnar.

They carried no lantern to betray their presence.
For the same reason, Hans Brikker would not dare
to bring one to the pen. He would be obliged to

[85]

wait for light enough from approaching day for what he meant to do.

Gunnar had his loaded musket slung across his shoulders. In the deep pocket of his rough woolen coat was the clip which was to be used in marking the pigs' ears. His father had expressly charged him and Astrid not to let themselves be seen until Brikker had his hands on a pig, and was about to mark it at the pen, or to carry it off to his own field and mark it there.

Brikker's pasture bordered Lars Nilsson's wood, and was separated from it by a rail fence. In this oak wood a number of pigs belonging to Lars had been allowed to roam for many months to fatten on the acorns. During this period several litters of young pigs had been born. None of these had their owner's mark as yet, and some of the older pigs still lacked it.

On the preceding day Gunnar had helped his father to pen up all these unmarked ones in the middle of the wood behind barriers of fallen branches and brush. This had been difficult to accomplish because of the obstinacy of the pigs, but working together, Lars and his son had succeeded at last in getting every one of them into the rude pen. These pigs were a valuable part of the stock of the Nilssons'

Astrid slipped through the darkness of her father's wood with Gunnar

small but flourishing farm.

A dense thicket, a few yards from the pen where the pigs lay snoring peacefully, offered Gunnar and Astrid an excellent covert. They concealed themselves in it and waited.

Thick dew showered from the leaves of the surrounding bushes upon Astrid's and Gunnar's head and shoulders. Their clothing and shoes became wet also.

Huddled close together they kept their eyes fixed in the direction from whence Brikker must come.

Gray light was stealing over the landscape when they discerned the Dutchman's stout unwieldy figure plodding across his pasture straight toward that part of the fence nearest to the pen. He was trundling a wheelbarrow containing a large empty sack.

Gunnar and Astrid exchanged glances. A few minutes more and they would catch the rascal dead to rights. They scarcely breathed as Brikker reached the fence, took down a sufficient number of rails in one spot to enable him to hoist his wheelbarrow over into the wood, climbed after it, and pushed the barrow to the very edge of the pen.

Sack in hand he scrambled awkwardly into the pen, threw down the sack and seized the nearest pig, an extra fine porker, to clip its ear. His plan was to mark each pig as his own, slip the heavy sack over its head, drag his prize to the wheelbarrow, and by means of that clumsy vehicle convey the heavy animal to the fence. There the pig was to be released from the sack, though upon Brikker's side of the fence. His mark upon any livestock found on his premises would be sufficient proof that it belonged to him.

He was on his knees, the clip in his hand and the struggling pig in position for marking, when suddenly Gunnar rose in the thicket, his musket aimed accurately at Brikker's broad back.

Just as the unfortunate pig in the Dutchman's grasp uttered a loud protesting squeal and started its rudely awakened companions to grunting vociferously in sympathy, Gunnar's imperative command struck on Brikker's ears like a thunderclap:

"Loose that pig instantly, Hans Brikker, or you'll get a bullet through your back."

Taken completely by surprise, Brikker cast a terrified glance behind him. It showed him Gunnar's determined face, flashing eyes, leveled musket; showed him Astrid also, watching him closely.

The clip fell from his hand and he let go involuntarily of the pig which he had clutched the tighter in his arms at the unexpected sound of Gunnar's voice. To deny what he had come for was impossible, but at least he would try to brazen the matter out.

He stood up, stiffened himself like a ramrod, and

clapped both arms flat to his sides. "These pigs have no mark on them," he shouted, his face red as a beet. "Unmarked pigs belong to nobody. I have as good a right to them as you. Besides that, I have the magistrate's permission to mark and claim any unmarked wild pigs that are roaming about in the woods."

"These are not wild pigs, as you know very well," rapped out Gunnar, stepping into the pen. "Nor is this a wood that belongs to no one. It is my father's property and every pig in it is his. They have been driven into this pen on purpose to be marked as his."

Brikker laughed scornfully. "This wood is mine by rights. His Excellency Petrus Stuyvesant granted it to me long years ago. That means that everything in it belongs to me, and unmarked pigs that trespass in it can be claimed by me."

Gunnar laughed back at him with equal scorn. "You never lived on your lands when they were first given you. You deserted them and the settlement almost at once, and ran away to Maryland to escape hard times. It was then that you lost your right to your grant and it was sold to my father by the authorities; he paid good money for it."

Astrid spoke accusingly from the other side of the barrier of branches. "You never would have come back at all, as everyone knows, if you had not been forced into it when His Excellency Petrus Stuyvesant demanded that Maryland should compel everybody who ran away from here to return."

"Let me have no impudence from a girl's tongue," shouted Brikker tartly. "What does she know about men's affairs?"

"Enough to tell the difference between the truth and falsehood," she retorted.

Brikker was opening his thick lips for another and more scathing volley, but Gunnar interrupted him brusquely. "There is to be no more talk now. That can take place before the magistrate. At this instant you will march out of this wood with empty sack and wheelbarrow unless you want a bullet from me." He placed his finger on the trigger, prepared to fire.

The risk of remaining was more than Hans Brikker cared to venture. He darted a glance of rage and helpless spite at the two who had caught him so neatly in his villainy. Then he snatched up his empty sack, clambered over the farther side of the pen as fast as his stocky legs and bulky frame would permit, and laid hold of his wheelbarrow which creaked dolefully as he made haste to the fence and got himself and it onto the other side upon his own land.

Gunnar and Astrid having seen him well away, turned their attention to the pigs. She helped to hold them while her brother put Lars' mark upon them.

When all, even the very smallest ones, were marked, he made a wide opening in the pen so that the pigs could pass out and roam the woods at will. The animals, venting a chorus of grunts and squeals, and pushing and shoving one another, ran past him and began to gobble acorns.

Gunnar put his clip into his pocket. "The next

thing," he said to his sister, "is to accuse the rogue before the magistrate. Father must do that, but we can bear witness to what happened here."

"When we do," Astrid warned him, "we must be most careful not to betray Elsa."

"Of course not," replied Gunnar.

CHAPTER IX

NO JUSTICE IS TO BE HAD in this place," stormed Gunnar. He was boiling over with indignation.

His father, Astrid, and he were walking away from the office of the magistrate before whom Hans Brikker had been arraigned, and before whom Gunnar and Astrid had given their testimony after Lars had made his accusation.

Brikker had stolidly denied the charge in every particular.

The magistrate had dismissed the case. "You have all your pigs, marked as yours, and you have acknowledged that none is missing," he had said to Lars in pronouncing his decision. "I cannot see that you have actually proved anything against this man, and his word is probably as good as yours. Make up between you your squabbles and your quarrels, and live in peace with one another."

With this advice he waved them out of his presence.

Hans Brikker had leered at them triumphantly as they were departing.

"On this occasion there has certainly been no justice," Lars granted to his son. He was hobbling along the New Castle street toward home, aided by an ash staff, for his ankle was still troublesome.

"The Long Finn promises that there shall be justice for everyone always, if we Swedes and Finns will only rise, with him as our leader, and throw off this English yoke," blurted out Gunnar boldly.

Lars rebuked him instantly. "How often must I tell you that I wish to hear nothing more about this Long Finn? He has come simply to stir up trouble for his own purposes."

[95]

Gunnar curbed himself, out of respect to his father, but Astrid, noting his sulky face, guessed that he would have said much if he had felt free to do so.

Long Finn's name was often mentioned nowadays in New Castle, and what he wished the Swedes and Finns to do was common talk among them. He and Hindrich Collmann had been going about persistently, making their fiery speeches and trying their best to stir up a revolt. It was sufficient to cause them to be arrested by the authorities, but they had a way of escaping from view at the crucial moment.

Rumor, which was quite correct, had it that the two took refuge among the Indians above and around Tinicum, whose language Collmann understood and spoke fluently. Whispers went from lip to lip among the Swedes and Finns that the "proud lady of Tinicum" was linked with them in sympathy if nothing more, but there was no proof of even that much, so far as was known.

Astrid was becoming increasingly uneasy about Gunnar, dreading lest he should be swept into this proposed revolt, if already he was not secretly allied to its leaders. Now and again, as he had today, he flared out into rebellious speech.

Lars was law-abiding and peaceable by nature. He was loyal to the oath of allegiance which he had given to the existing government when New Amstel was taken by the English and became New Castle in 1664. Therefore, he always checked his son promptly in these outbursts. He himself could easily recall the outrageous conduct and iniquitous rule of Hinoyossa, the last of the Dutch to govern the affairs of the town. Hinoyossa had been immeasurably worse than Lovelace and Captain Carr who represented him in New Castle.

Even had Lars approved of a revolt or been inclined to break his oath, he had too much hard common sense to see any prospect of a successful outcome for it. The English were greatly superior in numbers and in arms, and able to put down promptly by means of soldiers any insurrection before it could assume alarming proportions.

He was fully as disgusted and angry as Gunnar was at the dismissal of his complaint against Brikker as a matter of no consequence, merely because the Dutchman had not succeeded in his attempted theft. But he could control himself, and force himself to be content that he had at least sustained no loss.

Gunnar tramped back to hoeing in the cornfield, his brow lowering. Lars returned to his workbench in the kitchen, to whittle out a new wooden bowl for Karin who had broken hers that morning. Because his injured ankle still troubled him too much to let him work in the fields, and he could never pass his time in idleness, he kept himself busy at his workbench.

Astrid climbed to the loft of the storehouse to begin another yard of cloth. She had no more than seated herself upon the weaver's bench when she heard an imperious summons from below.

She went to the open window and looked down. The "proud lady of Tinicum" on her bay mare was in front of the storehouse waiting impatiently for attention to her call.

"What does Juffrou wish?" inquired Astrid politely.

"Someone to come at once to Printz Torp and weave for me. You will do well enough, so come. I expect to pay you." Armgart put this forth as though there could be no doubt that she would be obeyed instantly.

Astrid set her right on that point. "For that I should have to have my parents' consent, since my mother needs my help at home."

"Go and get it then," commanded Juffrou Armgart, "and bring me word quickly. I have no time to waste."

She sat her mare as though she were a sovereign

issuing commands to a subject. Astrid descended from the loft, crossed the grass to the house, and vanished indoors.

"To go to Printz Torp to weave? You?" exclaimed Ingeborg in dismay. "How can I possibly spare you? Who is to help me with the housework, the weaving, the twins, everything?"

Lars had set aside Karin's bowl and laid down his knife when Astrid delivered Juffrou's demand. He sat considering. When Ingeborg had spoken, he took up his work again. "The Juffrou expects to pay," he reminded her. "Astrid need not stay very long and a little extra money will not be a bad thing."

"Then I suppose I must consent," replied Ingeborg unwillingly, "but the Juffrou is no easy taskmistress. I need not tell you that."

"If she is too hard upon Astrid, that will end the business. The girl comes home then at once."

Ingeborg stepped out of the house and to Armgart Printz. "My daughter may weave for you, Juffrou," she said respectfully. "She is a good weaver. When do you wish her to come to Printz Torp?"

She waited, her hands twisted in her apron, sorry from the bottom of her heart as she looked into the arbitrary countenance of the woman above her that Lars had approved of Astrid's going.

"At once," replied Armgart. "She is to ride on the pillion behind me."

"If she is to stay, she must have clothes with her. Juffrou would need to wait until she packs a little bundle. Perhaps it would be better if my son brought her to you this evening." Ingeborg said this hoping that Juffrou Armgart might agree to the delay.

She was disappointed.

"Not at all," returned Armgart Printz shortly. "Have her pack her bundle immediately, and be quick about it. She is to ride along with me, as I said, and to stay until my weaving is done."

Within the half hour Astrid and her bundle were jogging behind Armgart over the Tinicum Road to Printz Torp.

Poor Astrid had no desire to go, nor any belief that she could be otherwise than uncomfortable, if not unhappy, under the same roof with this "proud lady of Tinicum" who sat haughty and coldly silent in the saddle in front of her.

With each step of the bay mare's hoofs the girl's heart sank lower, till it was difficult to restrain her tears. Homesick she would be, that much was inevitable. But what else? What else? she asked herself, in that strange place where she was to serve the imperious woman who was taking her thither.

While she was at Printz Torp she would know nothing of what went on at home: what Gunnar was doing; how Karin and Kirsten, who had wept bitterly when she had left them, were faring. She could not see her parents, nor would she see Eric, nor Elsa, for nobody knew how long. Heaviest upon her spirits weighed the uncertainty about Gunnar.

She felt miserably anxious and forlorn.

CHAPTER X

JUFFROU ARMGART'S HOUSE at Printz Torp, as Astrid saw it in the gathering dusk, was almost a mansion to the girl's inexperienced eyes. It was in fact only a plain farmhouse of the better sort and not by any means to be compared with Printzhof, which Johan Printz had built for himself on Tinicum Island when he was governor, surrounded with beautiful gardens and grounds, and fine orchards. The Printz Torp house was superior to the homes of the ordinary settlers along the river, but nothing more.

Printz Torp was on the mainland. Tinicum Island with all that was upon it had been sold, but was only partially paid for.

Old Olga in wooden shoes clumped through the hall of the Printz Torp house to throw open the front door. From the kitchen window she had seen her mistress arrive and alight, had seen that she brought a strange girl with her.

Juffrou Armgart swept in, followed by Astrid carrying her small bundle.

Olga Stark, filled with curiosity, fixed her shrewd little Finnish eyes upon Astrid, took note that she bore herself modestly, and wondered why she had been brought. She was promptly informed by her mistress.

"A girl to do my weaving. Yours has not pleased me. Take her to the loft where the loom is. She is to sleep in the small bed there. Tomorrow she is to begin work early."

An odd smile flitted across the old woman's countenance and was gone. She had told Juffrou Armgart on more than a few occasions why her own weaving had not been good, but her explanations had been cut off summarily. Very well, Juffrou would soon find out that this young girl could do no better than she (Olga) had done.

Armgart Printz, having given her orders, went on to her bedroom to bathe her face after the dusty ride from New Castle.

The loft to which Olga led Astrid was a gloomy place at night, with only a single tallow candle faintly to break its darkness. A great loom, several spinning wheels, a box bed in one corner, a solitary wooden stool, were the entire furnishings.

"The straw in the box bed is fresh, the covers are clean," mumbled Olga through almost toothless gums. "You can put your bundle on the floor. There are pegs and a rack to hang your clothes on, as you can see. You should want nothing more."

Astrid nodded silently and set down her bundle.

"Food is in the kitchen. I will show you the way," said Olga, picking up the candle and moving toward the stair that led below.

Loneliness and homesickness surged over Astrid in earnest as she left the loft and went down to the big kitchen with her guide to have her supper.

Rye porridge and milk, coarse bread, a scrubbed kitchen table, a small bench to sit upon, these were all familiar enough to her; but here there were no clamorous twins to be watched over and helped; no

Gunnar, laughing, joking, arguing. Above all there was no Lars, placid, kindly, sensible, firm; no Ingeborg, sweetly patient, capable, mothering her flock.

Only old Olga puttered about the hearth, shoveling her porridge into her withered mouth, stealing furtive though not unfriendly glances now and again at the girl across the table.

Juffrou Armgart ate alone in her dining hall, and Olga went back and forth from time to time to wait upon her.

Astrid felt tears stealing to her eyes. She wiped them away instantly and whenever Olga returned from the dining hall, she found the girl quietly eating her porridge.

After the meal she helped the old woman to clear away and restored the wooden bowls and plates and spoons to the wall racks as quickly as they were washed and wiped.

As soon as this was done, she took up the candle which Olga had extinguished when they came down from the loft, and relighted it. "Since I am to begin weaving early in the morning, I will go to bed now," she said.

Olga answered her good night, a knowing smile wreathing her lips when the girl's back was turned.

Dismay seized Astrid when she reached the loft,

set the candle on the stool, and surveyed the loom upon which she was expected to work. A single upward glance told her that she could never weave perfect cloth on such a loom, for the warp beam at the back of the loom was ill turned, uneven in its shape. From such a warp beam (or yarn roll) the threads would run off irregularly, spoiling the woof, making the cloth loose here, tight there, and full of loose threads.

She knew she must not even attempt to weave upon it. The "proud lady of Tinicum" would be sure to blame her for wasting the wool and ruining the cloth. She must go immediately and tell her that this loom was worthless but that if she could weave upon a good loom in Printz Torp, she would stay until the work was done. Otherwise she must go home. On the perfect loom in her father's loft she could weave excellent cloth for Juffrou, if she chose to bring her the wool for it.

Olga was not in the kitchen when Astrid re-entered it, but she did not wait on that account. She could find her way alone through the dimly lighted hall without trouble. Juffrou Printz would be apt to be sitting in one or other of the rooms on that floor.

She passed from the kitchen and advanced without hesitation. A light stronger than that which came from a candle in a holder on the wall was streaming from an open door.

Guided by this Astrid arrived at the door and looked in.

Armgart Printz sat in a big chair by the table. Papers were on the table which related to Tinicum Island. The man who had bought the island from her was in arrears with his payments, and she was considering how she could have him put off the island and get it back for herself.

She frowned when she saw Astrid standing in the doorway.

"What do you want?" she demanded harshly. "Your place is in the kitchen and in the loft."

"So it is, Juffrou," replied Astrid respectfully, "but it is necessary that I should tell you at once about the loom."

"The loom?" repeated Armgart sternly, beckoning her into the room. "Well, what about the loom?"

"It has a bad warp beam, Juffrou," Astrid informed her. "For that reason it would be altogether impossible to weave smooth even cloth upon your loom."

"Nonsense. If you know how to weave decently

you can do it on that loom. That is what I expect of you."

"No, Juffrou," insisted Astrid, her cheeks flushing under Armgart's irritated gaze, "neither I nor anyone could. If I am to weave for you at all, it must be on a well built loom here, or if you choose to send the wool, I can weave for you on our loom at home. That is for Juffrou to say."

"Always you peasants are full of excuses," Armgart flung at her contemptuously. "In the morning I will look at the loom myself, and see what can be done."

"Nothing can be done, Juffrou, except to replace the bad beam with a perfect one," Astrid assured her.

"I will decide that for myself," returned Armgart, waving her from her presence by an impatient authoritative gesture.

While she was saying this, there came a curious knocking on the house door: a series of raps—two short ones, a pause, a single heavier rap, a pause, and again two short ones. A signal, evidently, informing the mistress of the house as to who it was that knocked.

Armgart heard and understood. Her eyelids narrowed until they were mere slits through which her

flinty eyes could scarcely be seen. She had not expected that the person on the doorstep would make
his appearance this evening. Old Olga could be
trusted to open the door to him, but this girl must
not see him.

Astrid had heard the knocking and stopped as
she was about to pass from the room. "Shall I open
the house door for you, Juffrou?" she inquired oblig-
ingly.

"No! That is for Olga to do," Armgart answered
ungraciously. "Go to your bed in the loft at once,
and let me hear no more from you tonight. Go instantly."

Olga, in her wooden shoes, was already clacking
along the hall. As she passed Astrid obeying Juffrou
Armgart's order, she gave her a push, muttering,
"Get to the kitchen, or to the loft, as fast as you can.
What business have you poking around in this part
of the house?"

Just as Olga reached the door, the knocking was
repeated, slightly louder than before. Except for
that, it was precisely the same.

Astrid, at the end of the hall, stopped involuntarily
and glanced back over her shoulder.

The door was opening. A tall, handsome man
towered above the doorstone and stepped across the

sill with assurance. His piercing eyes looked straight to the farther end of the hall and perceived Astrid standing there as if fascinated, her gaze fixed upon him in undisguised surprise, her lips parted, her girlish figure held tensely.

He discerned her every feature distinctly in spite of the dim and flickering light from the candle in the wall sconce, and realized that she recognized him. Not by the faintest sign did he betray that he remembered her as the girl who had directed him to this very place many weeks ago.

Olga ushered him into the room where Armgart sat, large and important, filling the chair with her bulk. By the time the old woman had closed the door of the room upon the two as her mistress commanded, had turned and clumped down the hall again, Astrid had vanished and was in the loft overhead.

The startled girl needed no one to tell her that the man who had crossed the threshold of the house and was now closeted with Juffrou Printz, was Königsmarck, the Long Finn.

It was true then, beyond a doubt, she told herself, that Juffrou Printz had secret dealings with the man. The peculiar knocking, the haste on the part of Juffrou and Olga to get her out of the way before she could see who entered, were sufficient evidence of that.

Astrid set the candle in its iron holder upon the floor and sank down upon the stool. She was loth to be in a house to which the Long Finn came to plot with its mistress.

CHAPTER XI

LONG FINN, USHERED IN
to Juffrou Armgart, made the deferential bow which
he knew was expected of him. He had no especial
respect or liking for the "proud lady of Tinicum,"
but he never overlooked the fact that she could be
of use to him in the carrying out of his schemes,
whether or not she furthered them openly.

In any case, he could not afford to make a declared enemy of her. Unpopular though she was

among her own people, she had it in her power to acquaint the English of his plans and activities. Therefore, he intended to keep on her good side by flattering her vanity.

This evening she went so far as to bestow upon him a grudging smile, and extended her jeweled hand for him to kiss.

Long Finn touched his lips lightly to her clammy fingertips. He would gladly have been excused from this ceremony.

"What progress have you made recently?" inquired Armgart, when he had seated himself a short distance from her.

"That I will tell you presently, Juffrou," he replied, "but first I must speak to you of something else, must warn you."

"Must warn me?" she echoed, her sandy eyebrows lifted.

"Yes, Juffrou, I must warn you. You have brought a young girl into your house, a girl who may spy upon you and tell it about that I come to you here. That would not be well for either you or me, Juffrou, nor for the plans that we are making."

Armgart's laugh rang out. "A spy!" she scoffed. "Ridiculous! She is a harmless farmer's daughter. Her parents, Lars and Ingeborg Nilsson, are honest people

—Swedes. They would not betray Swedes."

"Do not forget this, Juffrou, Lars has absolutely refused to join in any attempt at revolt and has forbidden his son Gunnar to do so."

"Gunnar disobeys him. You told me yourself not long ago that he drinks in eagerly whatever you and Hindrich Collmann say."

"So he does, but he hides it from his parents. He has sworn to do so. It is not likely that his sister shares his feeling. Were I in your place, Juffrou, I would get rid of this girl as quickly as possible."

If there was one thing more than another that Armgart Printz wished to avoid, it was having her name coupled publicly with Long Finn's activities. Should the uprising be successful, then she would ally herself with it and him openly, but not before.

There might be a good deal of truth in what Königsmarck had just said about Astrid, and it would be best to send her away promptly. The cloth must be woven, of course, but the girl had offered to do it at her own home. The faulty beam in the loom would furnish a plausible excuse for sending her off.

Armgart rose from her carved chair. "I brought the Nilsson girl to Printz Torp to weave for me," she said, "but she has already complained of my loom. That affords me an excellent reason for having her go home. She can weave for me on her own loom in New Castle. In fact, she has suggested it. I will go to her at once, pretend to inspect the loom, and then tell her that she is to go early in the morning."

"You are wise," replied Long Finn, "and particularly in speaking to her without waiting. By this she will probably suppose that I have already left you, that my errand with you was brief, and that I met with no encouragement."

"You are sure that she saw you this evening?"

"As surely and as distinctly as she saw me one day, some weeks ago, when standing in the Bouwerie Wood she told me how to reach Printz Torp. This time she stopped at the end of your hall, turned, looked at me, and showed that she recognized me as a person whom she had seen before, though she may not yet know my name."

He had risen when Armgart rose.

"Sit down," she bade him as she moved toward the door. "When I return from speaking to the girl, I will hear what else you have to say."

The door closed after her, and Long Finn was left to himself.

In the loft Astrid was still crouched upon the stool, plunged in disquieting thoughts, her chin in her palms, her troubled eyes upon the bare boards of the floor.

The creak of the opening door at the bottom of the log stair, the ponderous figure of Juffrou Armgart Printz mounting the stair slowly, roused her and brought her to her feet in surprise at the unexpected visit.

Juffrou Armgart stepped out upon the loft floor without a word and raising her eyes to the warp beam, pretended to inspect it minutely.

Astrid waited in silence.

Several minutes passed while the mistress of Printz Torp scanned the beam and the other parts of the loom. Then she let her eyes come to rest upon the fair-haired girl, and spoke in even tones.

"There is something in what you have said about the warp beam. I can see that it has not been well made. Olga should have mentioned that to me long ago, but she is a stupid creature. My cloth must be of the best. Since you have a good loom at home, you may go back to it in the morning. Early, you understand. I will send you the wool as soon as I can spare a horse and a man to carry it. That will be impossible for me until later. For that reason you will have to walk home."

"That I shall not mind, Juffrou," replied Astrid

cheerfully, her spirits rising with the prospect of escaping from Printz Torp so soon.

"Why should you mind?" returned Armgart in-differently. "It is not more than twelve miles to New Castle, and you are a strapping healthy girl. See that you start early."

This injunction given, she descended the steep stair, leaving Astrid to rejoice over her good fortune in returning to her family, in leaving plots and schemes behind her. Oh, she would be early, early, on the Tinicum Road, she promised herself.

Now she must sleep. She undressed swiftly, blew out the candle, and lay down in the box bed. The long straw in the box rustled under the thick carpet-like rug that covered it. She settled down upon it, laid her head upon the hard bolster, and closed her eyes.

Whether or not the Long Finn talked late with the mistress of Printz Torp that evening, Astrid neither knew nor cared.

The sun was casting its first rays above the hori-zon when Astrid went down the loft stairs, carrying her bundle.

Olga, on her knees before the hearth, quickening the coals with the bellows to kindle the breakfast fire,

threw an inquiring glance at her, for Juffrou Armgart had not troubled to inform her servant that the
girl was to depart.

"What now?" she mumbled.

Astrid explained.

Olga laughed till her sides shook and her eyelids
squeezed together. "No one, not even I, can weave
decent cloth on such a loom. Juffrou knows that for
I have told her what was the matter over and over
again."

She got up from her knees, a tightly built, solid
little figure, round as one of her own rye loaves.

"You must eat before you go," she declared. "No
one travels well on an empty stomach. The porridge
is not cooked yet, but there is bread and there is

cheese. A meal can be made of those."

She laid two thick slices of bread and a wedge of cheese on the table, filled a wooden mug from a pitcher in the pantry and put it with the rest. "Here is milk, besides," she said, "and God bless it to you."

The Tinicum Road had no other living soul upon it when Astrid stepped out from Printz Torp. Bird songs, glistening dew, freshness of morning were there to cheer her. Two miles farther south she would pass through Finland with its scattered log houses. Five miles more and she would reach Fort Christina. A little over five miles more and she would be in New Castle.

There would be creeks and brooks to be crossed, but that she would not mind. She could wade at the fords or spring from rock to rock, and every step would bring her nearer home.

Mile upon mile she traversed, meeting no one. Occasionally she shifted her bundle from one hand to the other, but it was of no great weight and did not tire her.

She was still a few miles from home and was warbling a melodious Swedish ditty to beguile the way, when her attention was attracted by a small enclosure, surrounded by stakes, a stone's throw to the left of the road.

[119]

Curiosity drew her to it. She found it to be, as she had supposed, an old wolf-pit, built some years ago to entrap the ferocious wolves. In summer they roved singly, were cowardly, and slunk away from human habitations, but in winter they ventured boldly in packs to the edges of the settlements.

To rid themselves of this menace, the settlers dug wolf-pits, staked them round, and threw bait into the bottom. These pits were twelve feet or more deep, wider at the bottom than at the top, and stakes three or four feet high were driven into the ground closely all around the top edge. A wolf, lured by the scent of the bait, would leap over the stakes, fall into the pit, and be unable to escape from it. There he must stay until the hunters came and shot him.

Ever since the last wolf had been trapped in this pit which Astrid saw, there had been an opening in the barriers which surrounded it, made by the hunters in order to drag the dead wolf out of the pit after it had been killed.

That was long ago. The stakes were rotting now, and the ground about the edges of the pit was soft from recent rains. It was on this softened, yielding earth that Astrid stood, keenly interested in seeing how the pit was constructed.

She leaned forward slightly and in that instant the

treacherous ground caved under her weight. She seized the nearest stake to save herself, but it was rotten and broke in her hand. She lost her balance entirely and was precipitated into the depths of the pit.

Her bundle, reaching the bottom before she did, broke her fall to some extent and saved her from worse injury than a very heavy jarring and bruising of her body.

Severely shaken and dazed by the suddenness of what had occurred, she lay inert where she had struck. Dampness crept round her trembling form, for the pit dripped with moisture.

When she had recovered sufficiently to raise her head and scan the uncompromising slopes which surrounded her, she realized with a sickening pang that there was no hope of rescuing herself. The sides of the pit, sloping cone-like toward the top, offered her no foothold.

She had only the slender chance that someone passing along the Tinicum Road might be attracted by her outcries and come to her aid. Otherwise there was no telling how long she might be captive in this pit.

Her parents believed her to be safe at Printz Torp. Juffrou Printz would consider that she had reached her home. By the time it was discovered that she was lost, the hue and cry was raised and search made, what might she not have suffered?

And would they find her at all where she lay hid? Would they hear her when she cried out?

She gathered herself together, stood up, and began to shout, lustily, determinedly, insistently. Her voice ascending from the bottom of the pit, floated muffled into the forest aisles and toward the Tinicum Road.

No answer came, nor did any feet draw near the wolf-pit.

CHAPTER XII

Hours passed, and Astrid, worn out and discouraged, was forced to cease her hoarse cries for help. In place of these, she strained her ears for the sound, however faint, of approaching feet. When she heard those, she would cry out again. Until then it would be useless.

The sun was high in the heavens when her sharpened sense detected what seemed to her to be the footsteps of a man, advancing slowly down a trail which ran into the forest from the Indian country in the northwest. Traders often used this trail in going back and forth to exchange goods with the savage tribes.

Astrid waited in silence for a few moments, to make sure that she had not been mistaken. Her throat was raw from continued shouting. She must not waste her waning power to use her voice.

Stronger, more distinct became the footfalls on the trail. Not those of moccasined feet, but feet cased in thick leather and sturdy soles. They were not far off.

"Help! Help!" she shrieked at the top of her lungs imploringly. "Help! Help! Here in the wolf-pit! Help, oh, help!" she cried again.

Although she received no answer, she could tell that the person was moving faster and was coming straight to the pit. She gave one final guiding call and waited.

The feet halted at the pit's edge. Astrid gazed upward full of hope.

Hope changed swiftly to despair, for peering down upon her was a countenance full of malice, and she heard the spiteful tones of Hans Brikker.

"So, our meddlesome Swedish wench makes her own punishment! That is good. May it last long. While she takes it, she can be remembering that Hans

Brikker saw her, that Hans Brikker knows where she is, but that Hans Brikker will never tell where she can be found. Let her folks hunt. Let them wonder till they are tired. And let her scream for help till her lungs burst."

Astrid flashed cold scorn upon him before she turned her back upon his unwieldy bulk, his sneering, thick-lipped, coarse-featured countenance. She would not answer him by a single word.

He could not abandon her to her wretchedness without more railings and insults, nor without cruelly enjoying in her presence her unhappy plight.

She sat down upon her bundle. Not once did she lift her eyes to him. Not one syllable passed her set lips.

Brikker was in no haste to leave, but at last he was compelled to give up gloating over her and go about the business which waited for him in New Castle.

When he was gone Astrid crouched down upon the floor of the pit, her face hidden upon her bundle, her head on her clasped hands. She rallied her sinking courage, prayed that she might not be utterly forsaken, that help would be sent her.

Hunger and thirst took hold of her. She had eaten early. It was long past noon. She could do nothing but cry aloud from time to time as the hours crept by. This she did, but always in vain.

She gave up at last, rested her head on her bundle and lost herself and her misery in sleep.

Late that afternoon Ingeborg was stirring dye in the dye-pot. She was preparing to color hanks of wool for the winter's weaving.

A figure darkening the doorway made her glance in that direction. She saw Olle Palsson, one of the Finnish laborers from Printz Torp, entering. He carried an enormous bundle, went with it to the long bench and set it down.

"The wool from Juffrou Printz," he announced gruffly.

Ingeborg paused in her stirring of the dye. "The wool?" she repeated. "What wool?"

"For the weaving that your daughter is to do for Juffrou," replied the Finn.

Ingeborg stared at him in her astonishment. "My daughter!" she exclaimed. "My daughter is at Printz Torp doing Juffrou's weaving there. What do you mean, Olle?"

"Your daughter has not been at Printz Torp since very early this morning. The loom there is no good, so Juffrou sent her home on foot. The wool comes now."

"Astrid was sent home alone?" demanded Ingeborg.

"Alone," replied Olle.

"But she has not got here. She should have been at home many hours ago."

Olle shrugged his shoulders. "Girls often linger by the way," he affirmed.

Ingeborg spoke rapidly and with rising indignation. "Not my Astrid. Some misfortune has befallen her. Juffrou Printz had no right to send her off in such a manner. It is an outrage."

For this Olle had no answer. His mistress was a hard woman and he could not deny it.

"Search will have to be made at once," went on Ingeborg, pale with anxiety. "God alone knows what may have happened to my child! From wild beasts, from Indians! Run, Olle, to the field and send Lars and Gunnar to me. You can see for yourself that I can't leave the twins."

Olle was willing to do that much, and took himself off in a hurry on the horse which he had left standing outside the gate.

Lars and Gunnar, filled with alarm by what Olle told them, left their farm implements in the furrows and made haste to the house. They heard what Ingeborg had to say, and then Gunnar ran to the barn and hitched up the farm wagon. Lars put into it a coil of rope, a lantern, and an ax. Ingeborg added a parcel of food and a thick blanket.

"Brandy may be needed," muttered Lars, and thrust a flask of it into his deep coat pocket.

"We will search first along the Tinicum Road," he told his wife. "That is the way she would have followed, and not a trail through woods."

They set out, Lars driving the horse slowly, while Gunnar looked along the outskirts of the wood, scanning trails and thickets in every direction, and calling Astrid's name.

They had not gone far when they were overtaken by Eric Helm, breathless from running. He had happened to meet Olle at the town end of the Tinicum Road, and Olle had blurted out, "The Nilsson girl is lost in the woods somewhere between Printz Torp and New Castle. Her father and Gunnar have gone to hunt for her."

Eric had needed nothing more to spur him to join in the search.

"You keep close to the road," he said to Gunnar. "I will go straight forward, too, but farther in. If we do not find her before we get to Printz Torp, we can use a different plan if your father thinks best."

"If only she has not been carried off by Indians," said Gunnar in smothered tones.

"Do not think of that," begged Eric. "Remember that the Indians have always been friendly to us Swedes. They have never harmed any of us since our earliest settlements."

Gunnar took comfort from this.

Slowly they proceeded—Eric among the thickets, Gunnar from the roadside, Lars from the wagon—calling as they went. Lars was able from his elevation to see farther into the forest than his companions.

None of them descried the least trace of the one they sought. Strangely enough, none of them thought of the possibility of her having met with disaster from some old wolf-pit. They had no reason to suppose that she would have approached any such place. There was nothing to take her to it. Besides that, it was fenced in.

Had Astrid been awake when they were in the vicinity of the wolf-pit, she must inevitably have heard their voices. But she had fallen into the heavy sleep of exhaustion, and being so many feet below the surface of the ground with the pit walls bending together over her head, their voices were blurred and did not rouse her.

They did no more than cause her to dream uneasily, a vague dream in which it seemed to her she heard her name shouted far off in familiar voices which she could not definitely recognize.

So the three searchers moved on toward Fort Christina, and when she woke and cried aloud again, they were too distant from her to catch the sound at all.

Arrived at Fort Christina, Gunnar inquired of a soldier near the sally-port whether anyone had seen Astrid go by. The church to which the Nilssons went regularly every Sunday was in the fort enclosure, and the garrison knew her by sight.

The soldier answered promptly, "Yes, but that was many hours ago, early this morning in fact. I was on sentry at the time, and noticed her, and that she was alone."

"That means that we must go back," said Lars, and turned the horse's head, but paused to inquire, "Have there been Indians about today?" The soldier would be able to give reliable information as to that for Indians came often to the fort to trade.

"Not for several days," returned the soldier, "at least not at the fort."

What he said did not altogether reassure Lars and his companions, since Indians might easily have been hunting in the woods near by without going to the fort. Moreover drunken Indians or Indians in quest of "firewater" were often seen around New Castle and the woods surrounding it.

Dusk was thickening as they turned back. Gunnar lighted the lantern and hung it at the tail of the wagon.

Soon Eric lifted it off, saying, "If I carry it in my hand and go farther into the wood, perhaps its beams may penetrate to Astrid if she is lying hurt or wounded anywhere, or it may rouse her if she is sick or faint. Then if our voices reach her, she may gather strength enough to answer."

His tones were despondent but he would not give up hope. Lars and Gunnar were as dejected as he but they, like himself, were determined to seek until they found her.

Therefore they redoubled their shouts, taking turns at it, so that there would be no confusion of sounds, so that her name would ring distinctly along and into the forest glades.

With the approach of night Astrid waked, but waked to fear of worse than being alone and at the bottom of the wolf-pit. She knew that she would not be molested by humankind of ill intent where she was. The depth and construction of the pit would guard her from those.

But wild beasts prowled at night. A wolf, a wild-cat, guided by her scent, might leap into the pit to seize upon her there. Without means of defense, faced by one of these, she would have no chance at all for life—a hideous thought, a hideous fear, which made her heart contract and her flesh creep.

She knew that to cry aloud after darkness fell would profit her nothing. She no longer listened for human footsteps. Her ears were keyed instead for rustlings in the thickets, for the padding footfalls of beasts.

Night closed down; blacker it seemed to her than she had ever known it.

Then it was, when despair and dread grew every instant stronger, that she heard her name called as though from a long distance off.

"Astrid! Astrid!"

She could barely discern it but presently she knew she was not mistaken, and her heart leapt in her breast.

"Astrid!" This time it was nearer, and in Eric's voice.

She rose on tiptoe, threw back her head, and sent her answer upward. "Here I am."

"Astrid! Astrid!" That was Gunnar, nearer.

Eric was determined to seek until he found her

The rumble of a cart, and from it her father exhorting her. "Astrid! Keep calling, girl. Keep calling, so that we can find you."

"I am here, here in the wolf-pit," she shrieked again and again.

Now they came fast and faster—Eric, casting the lantern beams to right and left to locate the pit, Gunnar at his heels, Lars following upon the highway. All three were looking, looking intently, for the posts which they knew would be their infallible guide to the enclosure.

Deliverance at hand, Astrid's voice failed her utterly, but she had no need to use it, for Eric, Gunnar, Lars had spied the posts, had rushed to the pit, were at its edge.

She raised her tear-wet eyes to theirs, lifted her arms, but could not speak.

"One moment more, my dear child," Lars encouraged her. "In a moment or two—and you shall be out of this hole."

He spoke to Gunnar: "Fetch the rope from the cart, boy. We shall have to use it to pull her out."

But Gunnar was already halfway to it. He brought it, and under his father's direction, tied one end of it securely to the trunk of a near by tree.

Lars made thick knots along the length of the rope,

spaced so that Astrid would have foothold and hand-hold by means of them.

Eric held the lantern while this was done. Then the rope was lowered, and Astrid, grasping it, was tugged steadily upward by Lars and Gunnar, and brought out on to safe ground.

She stumbled and turned faint when she reached it.

Lars caught her, snatched the flask from his pocket, and poured a little brandy between her lips. It burned like fire as it went down, but it revived her.

They would have carried her to the cart, but she would not have it so. They supported her to it and made her lie down on the folded blanket, her bundle under her head. Lars urged food upon her and she ate gladly.

Eric hung the lantern at the cart tail and mounted to a seat beside Lars. Gunnar unfastened the rope from the tree and when he had coiled it, flung it into the cart and sat upon it.

As the cart began to jog toward New Castle, Lars spoke to his daughter over his shoulder. "The 'proud lady of Tinicum' shall hear what I think of this, my child." His tones were biting. "As for Hans Brikker, he is a beast."

CHAPTER XIII

Lars Nilsson stood be-
fore Armgart Printz in her great-room at Printz
Torp. He had declined the seat which she indicated
he might take. He chose to be on his feet while he
had his say, and he was speaking at length.

There was a large bundle on the floor beside him,
which he had set down when he entered.

His uncompromising gaze was fixed on Armgart.
She felt the stern reproof of it, though outwardly she

maintained her arrogant unconcern.

"You think of no one but yourself, Juffrou. If you had sent my daughter home properly, on horseback, with one of your farm men, as you should have done, no harm would have come to her. You sent her alone and on foot, early in the morning. If she was to walk the distance, at least one of your men should have walked with her to take care of her."

Armgart shrugged her shoulders indifferently. "What are twelve miles to a stout girl? If your girl has not sense enough to keep from tumbling into wolf-pits, whose fault is it?"

Lars reddened angrily. "There is no girl in these colonies who has more good sense than my Astrid. An accident can happen to anyone, even to yourself, Juffrou. How did you know that she might not be harmed by an Indian or by some wild beast? Such things have occurred before this. Besides that, if she had not been alone, there would have been someone to give warning, or to get help for her."

His indignant eyes continued to accuse her, but Armgart refused to be stirred to any compunction for her neglect.

"Say what you please, the girl was careless," she retorted. "She had no business to be poking around wolf-pits. She should have kept straight to the road."

"That a girl notices what is unfamiliar to her and feels a little curiosity about it, is not to be wondered at. She had no reason to suppose that the earth would cave under her so that she could not keep her balance, and that she would fall in. Besides, how could she know that the stakes were as rotten as they are? The fact remains that you should have sent her home safely."

He raised aloft the bundle of yarn which had been resting on the floor at his feet. "As things have turned out, here is your yarn, Juffrou. Get your weaving done where you can. It shall not be done by my daughter."

Armgart bridled stiffly. "You are a fool, Lars Nilsson. I would have paid her good money for her weaving."

"Money does not pay for everything, Juffrou," returned Lars imperturbably, taking a long step and depositing the bundle directly in front of her.

Armgart glared resentfully after his sturdy figure as he turned and left her. "Impudent Swede," she muttered. "If Sweden wins back these Delaware settlements, I shall have some power given me for my part in it. Then I shall teach him his place."

She asserted this with considerable confidence, for the persistent efforts of Long Finn and his confederates were beginning to bear encouraging fruit. A number of the more prosperous Swedes and Finns, as well as the poorer settlers, were listening with increasing favor to the seditious speeches which were poured into their ears. The wilder and unruly element had yielded promptly to the influence of Evert Hindricksson at Crane Hook.

It was known to them all now that Juffrou Armgart Printz was secretly in sympathy with the proposed insurrection, and equally known to them that her name was not even to be whispered in this connection until she herself gave open consent. No one criticized this. She was a woman. She had much to lose if the rising was not successful. She was a clever person who might be of great use to the cause. They would be careful not to betray her.

One evening, a few days after Lars had expressed his mind freely to Juffrou Printz, Gunnar was oddly restless at the supper table. Again and again he seemed moved to speak of something, then to put sudden check upon himself and withhold it.

Each time Astrid looked at him inquiringly, but he either turned his head aside without meeting her eyes, or occupied himself briskly with his porridge as though that were his sole concern.

When the meal was over, instead of lingering a

while to play with the twins, he hugged them to him almost fiercely, then pushed them gently away. Rising from his stool, he leaned over his mother and kissed her, laid his palm for an instant on his father's broad shoulder, which was a most uncommon action on his part, and stroked Astrid's hair tenderly before he picked up his musket and strolled off toward the Bouwerie Wood in the sunset light.

Hours slipped by. Lars and Ingeborg rested on the long bench outside the house, he with his pipe, she with her knitting, as usual. Astrid worked in her garden. Karin and Kirsten chased one another up and down the paved walk.

Bedtime came and there had been no sign of Gunnar.

Lars knocked the ashes from his pipe, stood up, and stretched himself. "Gunnar tries my patience lately," he complained. "He should have been at home by now."

"That he should," agreed Ingeborg, folding up her knitting and following her husband indoors.

It was the hour at which shutters and the outer door were always closed and barred, and the fire covered to prevent dangerous sparks from flying about in the night.

Lars paced the kitchen back and forth, back and

forth, unwilling to drop the bar across the closed door.

Astrid and Ingeborg waited too, pretending to busy themselves with trifling tasks, though actually they were listening for Gunnar's familiar step on the paved walk.

A footfall was heard at last, but it was not Gunnar's. It and the knock that followed were Eric Helm's.

Lars flung open the door in answer to the knock. "Come in, come in, Eric," he said to the figure on the doorstep. "What brings you to us at this hour?" By instinct he grasped that something connected with Gunnar was the occasion of Eric's visit, though he did not say so.

The three searched the lad's face as he entered. In it they thought they discerned a reluctance, a sense of a painful duty which had fallen on him to perform; these, and an overpowering sympathy.

For the space of a minute Eric remained silent, as though words refused to come.

Those who waited felt an icy chill fall upon them, a premonition of impending disaster.

Lars could not endure the delay. "Speak, Eric, in God's name," he said.

"Gunnar," began Eric, then stopped as though it

were too difficult for him to go on.

"Gunnar—yes, Gunnar—" urged Lars painfully.

"Gunnar?" whispered Ingeborg, twisting her apron into knots. "What about our Gunnar?"

Astrid pressed both hands to her heart to still its wild beating. Her large eyes implored Eric to say quickly what had happened to her brother.

Eric nerved himself. "Less than half an hour ago Gunnar met me by the river where I was beaching my boat. He begged me to come and tell you that he was going at once to Crane Hook to train under Evert Hindricksson, and to join the Long Finn; to say that he was going, and would not be home again."

"Not be at home again!" echoed Astrid and Ingeborg under their breath. They gazed at Eric, stupefied by the shock.

"To Crane Hook—to Evert Hindricksson—to join the Long Finn!" Lars murmured, dumbfounded. He had never believed that his son, despite rebellious talk and resentment of English authority, would take such a step as this.

"I begged him not to, said everything I could," deplored Eric, his head bowed, his fingers tensely clasped, "but it was altogether useless. He was like a flint. I could do nothing whatever with him. The Long Finn, Evert Hindricksson, yes, and Hindrich

Collmann have swept him completely away."

"That I should have lived to see this!" groaned Lars. "That my son should disobey me and bring such disgrace upon us! Never would I have believed it possible."

He sank down upon the long bench clutching his forehead. He had taken the oath of allegiance to Great Britain years ago, had kept it loyally. Now Gunnar, his only son, not yet of age, would be counted as a traitor, would be seized and punished as a traitor.

In Lars' estimation, to Lars' high standards of honor, nothing worse could have befallen. He could have seen Gunnar die in any good and righteous cause, and though it would have been a cruel grief, he could have been proud of him and mourned him without shame.

But to have this son of his forsake home and family, cast off obedience to established authority at home and abroad, to cut himself off from honorable law-abiding people in order to link himself to a desperado and to this mischief-making stranger, was more than Lars could endure. It was made all the harder because he was firmly convinced that Long Finn was a worthless fellow and an impostor, who had no proof to offer that what he said was true.

"Gunnar with Evert Hindricksson!" wailed Ingeborg, tears streaming down her cheeks. "Our Gunnar with such a rascal! Gunnar separated from decent people!"

Astrid, crushed by her parents' grief and by her own, laid her cold fingers on the sleeve of Eric's rough fishing coat. "Gunnar will stay at Crane Hook?" she asked faintly.

"Who knows?" replied Eric, deeply moved by her distress. "At any time he may go wherever the Long Finn is."

"Where is that?"

"It would be hard to say. Long Finn appears and disappears. Sometimes he is at Crane Hook with Hindricksson. Sometimes he is in the forests or among the Indians around Tinicum. Sometimes he is hidden by the Swedes. He even ventures into New Castle, though seldom by day. He does not risk being arrested by showing himself openly and speaking where officers of the law could hear him and seize him."

Lars raised his head. "I shall not wait for Gunnar to leave Crane Hook. Tomorrow morning I shall go there and bid him come home at once. He is not of age. I still have a right to command him."

"Do not go, father," pleaded Astrid. "Let me go

in your stead. Eric will take me, and I will talk to Gunnar and beg him to come home."

Lars shook his head decidedly. "No, Astrid. This is not a girl's business. I am the one who can speak with authority."

"It is because you will speak in that way that I ask you to let me go. If you command him, he may answer you in words for which he will always be sorry, and which will hurt you to remember. It does not matter what he says to me, and he may listen, may return. Let me go."

"Let her go," implored Ingeborg, for she, too, dreaded what father and son might say to one another, dreaded a breach which might never be healed.

"Let Astrid go," urged Eric. "I will take care of her. Depend upon it."

Beset by them all, Lars finally gave in, though with very bad grace. He granted the truth of what Astrid had said, and it was that alone that won his consent.

"Meet me at the wharf by Fort Casimir when the clock strikes seven," Eric bade Astrid. "I shall be waiting there with the boat."

"Before the clock strikes I shall be there," she answered.

[145]

Eric took his leave, and Lars dropped the bar across the door.

They sought their wall beds, Astrid, Ingeborg, Lars, crushed by the knowledge that Gunnar's bed in the loft overhead was empty, and that for the first time in his life he whom they loved would not come home to seek it.

CHAPTER XIV

ASTRID HAD SOME CON-
fidence in her power to influence Gunnar in this
crisis. He had always made it plain that she was very
dear to him and that he set much store by her good
opinion and approval, although she was younger
than he by several years.

If only she could see him face to face, he might
yield to her persuasions and all might yet be well.
Therefore hope filled her as she and Eric rowed

toward Crane Hook.

She had made Eric take an extra pair of oars so that she could help with the rowing, and they could thus reach their destination with greater speed.

They left New Castle in a drizzle of rain, but as they approached Crane Hook the skies grew lighter. By the time they had beached their boat, the sun was shedding a watery beam over the small settlement and the creeks and swampy land around Fort Christina on the other side of Christina Creek.

Eric stepped from the boat and Astrid was about to follow him, but he waved her back. "No, Astrid, stay in the boat. I should not like to have you go where you might meet some of Hindricksson's rough fellows. If I meet them, it will not matter. I shall find Gunnar and bring him to you. He surely will not refuse me. Here you can speak privately."

Astrid saw the sense of it. She sat down again in the boat while Eric made haste to find Gunnar.

Gulls soared and dipped around her, screaming harshly and busy with their morning fishing. The Jersey shore was blotted out by mists. A sailboat anchored in the river swayed with the motion of the tide from the bay.

Alone with these, Astrid pondered the words which she must use to have the most weight with

Gunnar. She must choose them well.

Her thoughts were broken in upon by the unexpected appearance of a man advancing rapidly from the hamlet of Crane Hook to a rowboat moored to a stake a few yards away.

He was of rugged Finnish type and features. His face in every line bore witness to the wild tempestuous fighting life he had led. He carried his head belligerently, his eyes challenged, his walk was a swagger. A short jacket, open from the throat down, swung impudently from his shoulders.

Astrid recognized him at once as the desperado, Evert Hindricksson. She would have given much to have Eric with her now for she feared Hindricksson might address her insolently.

He showed no intention of doing so at first, but went directly to his boat and bent to untie it from the stake.

She was congratulating herself on her escape, when all at once he wheeled, his hand still on the boat rope, the boat not yet loosed.

His bold eyes pierced her through and through. His derisive laughter floated to her. "You've come to fetch your brother home, no doubt. Don't think that he will go with you. He has shaken off leading-strings for good. He has bigger things to do now than to plow and hoe upon a farm."

She did not answer him.

Hindricksson let fall the rope and marched over to her. A shudder ran through her for she feared what he might do. He was lawless, evil, and she had ample cause to dread him. Many a tale she had heard of his misdeeds at Upland before he was banished thence. He was no better here at Crane Hook, perhaps.

He made no attempt to touch her, however, but glared into her frightened eyes. "Understand this," he bellowed, "and let it be once and for all: Gunnar Nilsson will not go home, will not listen to your silly words nor care for your silly tears. He follows the Long Finn, Hindrich Collmann, and me."

Hindricksson tapped himself triumphantly on the chest at his last word. "*And me*," he reiterated, "*Evert Hindricksson. I will teach him to fight.*"

Astrid spoke boldly. "Gunnar is not of age. He should obey his father until he is. And after that he could well heed his father's advice, for Lars Nilsson is a good man and a wise one."

"A good man! A wise one! Bah! Let him keep his goodness and his wisdom to himself. Gunnar is with me." Hindricksson walked from her to his boat, freed it from the stake, sprang in, and rowed upstream.

Astrid sighed her intense relief at his departure.

Neither of them had observed that Hans Brikker had paused in passing by, unseen, and was looking and listening from behind a screen of bushes. He was on a trading expedition to Fort Christina. A couple of fine beaverskins were in a pack on his shoulders. These he would exchange for merchandise to be had at the trading post at the fort.

The sight of Astrid having speech with the notorious Evert Hindricksson brought an ugly sparkle to his eyes. It vexed him that he could not hear a syllable of what was said between them, being a little too far away for that. Nevertheless they were together. He would make use of that fact when he saw fit.

When Astrid was alone again, he took good care that she did not perceive him creeping stealthily from bush to bush till he was quite out of her range of vision.

Eric returned at last, and Gunnar with him.

On Gunnar's face was a defiant expression, foreign to it.

Astrid's heart sank. How was she to penetrate this armor which he had assumed since he had cast off his old life, his old ties of affection?

She had left the boat when she saw him approaching. Now she went close to him, laid her arms about his shoulders, gazed lovingly into his gloomy eyes.

Eric stood well apart, leaving them to themselves.

"Gunnar, dear Gunnar," began Astrid, and stopped. The words that she had intended to speak died away on her lips.

Gunnar returned her look somberly. "What have you come to say, Astrid? What is there to say? I sent my message last night by Eric. I can add nothing to it, take nothing from it."

Astrid spoke earnestly and softly. "Gunnar, you are breaking our father's heart."

"Let him join us; let him follow the Long Finn. Then his heart will not break."

Her eyes never wavered from his though tears filled them. "Our father is an honest and an honorable man. He obeys the laws. What he swears to, he holds fast to. He gave his oath to the English. He will never break it. His oath binds you, his son, binds me, binds all his family. You are not of age. He is responsible for you. You should not disobey him, should not bring shame and disgrace upon him, upon our mother, upon us all."

Gunnar averted his eyes and turned away his head. Her arms he did not shake off. He could not go that far.

Her voice went on pleadingly. He could not close

Gunnar averted his eyes and turned away his head

his ears to it, but his jaws were obstinately fixed.

"When you are of age you will be at liberty to choose for yourself, to go your own way for good or for bad. But not now, Gunnar, not now. Evert Hindricksson is an evil man, an evil companion for you. Come away from him. Leave the Long Finn. Come home."

Gunnar's expression did not change. "Save yourself and me pain, Astrid," he bade her impatiently. "I cannot heed you, will not go with you. I have made my choice and I shall not alter it. If my father cannot see the dawn of a good day for us Swedes along the Delaware, that is no reason why I should be blind, why I should not help to bring it in."

"It is you who are blind, dear Gunnar," she replied, lifting a trembling hand to his cheek. She saw plainly that her influence had failed, that there was nothing more that she could do.

At her touch on his cheek Gunnar's countenance softened. He kissed her affectionately, wiped the tears from her eyes with a gentle hand. "Give over crying, Astrid," he said. "Some day, perhaps soon, you will be glad that I stayed with Königsmarck."

Astrid shook her head sorrowfully. She could not answer because of sobs, rising thick and fast, which she was determined to restrain.

Gunnar lifted her arms from around his neck. "Take her home, Eric," he called to his friend, and held her out to him. "She must not stay here any longer."

Astrid went disconsolately. Gunnar strode off resolutely to the hamlet at Crane Hook.

Astrid did not pick up her oars until Eric had rowed almost a mile downstream. She was cruelly disappointed, her hopes blasted. She hid her face upon her knees, still holding down the sobs that shook her, but her tears flowed fast.

Eric sat silent, bending steadily to his oars. He ached with sympathy for her, but he respected her grief and would not intrude upon its privacy by a single word.

CHAPTER XV

A WEEK CREPT BY.

Lars worked doggedly on his farm, shoulders squared, lips and jaws set grimly. He had to accomplish the bulk of what two men had done hitherto. Ingeborg took on as many of the household duties as she could possibly manage, so that Astrid could assist her father to some extent in the fields. But when harvesting must be done, Gunnar's help would be sorely missed.

Lars Nilsson's once placid countenance no longer radiated contentment. Ingeborg and Astrid had no heart to sing the ancient folksongs over their work. Karin and Kirsten pounded the table with their wooden spoons at mealtimes, wept loudly, and refused to be comforted because Gunnar was not there.

Whether Astrid raked or turned the hay in the meadow, whether she hoed corn, sat at the loom, tended the twins, or lifted her mother's burdens, her thoughts and imagination circled incessantly around Gunnar. She wondered where he was now, what he was doing.

Only rarely could she slip away for a brief moment with Elsa, and pour into her sympathetic ears the anxieties about Gunnar which beset her. She spoke of these to her parents as little as possible. They were weighed down by their own distress. She could not lighten it; she would not add to it.

In New Castle things appeared to move as quietly as usual, though a steady undercurrent of spying went on which none of the inhabitants suspected.

There was little that Hans Brikker did not ferret out, and he made an excellent profit by selling to the government authorities any information he picked up which could be of use to them.

Practically every evening he spent a couple of

hours in the tavern, apparently indulging innocently in a pot of ale. This was merely a cover for his business of listening to whatever was said by those who frequented the tavern, and he watched furtively everyone who came and went in the taproom.

Whatever information of value he gained, he took directly to Captain Carr who despatched it by his messenger to Governor Lovelace in New York. Carr paid Brikker as much as he considered each piece of information was worth.

Brikker did not confine his spying activities to the tavern. Whenever he went abroad in any direction he kept eyes and ears open for grist to his mill. He had discovered many details in relation to Long Finn and those co-operating with him. He had not overlooked the fact that Gunnar Nilsson had become one of these, nor did he forget that he had seen Astrid talking with Evert Hindricksson at Crane Hook. It elated him that besides putting money in his purse, he would be able, when he saw fit, to wreak a private revenge upon Lars Nilsson and his family.

Lately he had gained an important asset to his purposes in the person of Running Weasel, a Minquas Indian.

Fleet of foot, crafty, and none too scrupulous as to whom he accommodated, this Indian often acted as a runner or messenger, carrying letters and messages for anyone who required such services.

Hans Brikker had gained a strong hold upon Running Weasel through the savage's unquenchable thirst for "firewater." This thirst he was unable to gratify in a legitimate way for, at the request of a prominent Indian chief who saw the havoc wrought among his people by strong drink, the sale of liquor to the Indians had been restricted by law.

Brikker had no hesitation whatever in supplying Running Weasel with brandy or rum in order to gain any important information which the Indian could furnish.

Now that Long Finn and Hindrich Collmann were made welcome among the tribes along the Delaware, and were given refuge from danger among them, the Dutchman became increasingly willing to oblige Running Weasel.

One evening he was taking a mug of foaming ale at a table in the taproom of the tavern. The bench which he occupied was less than a yard from the open door and he faced the street.

The taproom was full of customers, served or being served according to their individual tastes. Each intent upon his own affairs, none of them paid any attention to Hans Brikker. He was not popular and was in the habit of drinking alone.

This evening his mug was partly emptied and he was taking the remainder of his ale slowly, when he noticed the figure of a savage passing before the door. He passed and repassed several times.

The fourth time he stood still, his naked arm and curved palm raised to the level of his brow. It was Running Weasel, giving the sign agreed upon between him and Brikker when he had something of consequence to communicate.

Their eyes met and then the Indian stepped out of sight.

Brikker finished his ale promptly, paid his reckoning, and left the tavern in his ordinary leisurely manner.

He was scarcely out of range of the mellow light streaming from the tavern door when he quickened his pace.

In a narrow lane which led from the Strand to the river, he found Running Weasel waiting for him in a dark recess between two sheds belonging to a warehouse. The Indian's tawny body, naked except for his loincloth and the moccasins on his feet, made him almost invisible in the darkness.

He displayed a packet to Brikker. "From Long Finn," he said, "for his white brother, Jan Stalcop."

Brikker's eyes glittered. Jan Stalcop, a well-off Swede, was one of the principal men who favored Königsmarck. He was about to seize the packet avidly, but Running Weasel withheld it.

"Firewater," he demanded. "When Running Weasel has that, his Dutch brother can have the letters."

Hans Brikker was prepared. Lodged in his capacious pocket was a large flask, full to the brim with extra strong brandy. He drew it forth and exchanged it for the coveted packet.

Running Weasel unstopped the flask and took a long pull at the contents. "Ugh!" he grunted in delight, and vanished forthwith in the direction of the woods beyond the town.

Brikker made haste to Fort Casimir to lay his prize in the hands of Captain Carr. The fort was crumbling into ruins, but a garrison was still maintained there and Carr had his quarters in the fort enclosure.

When Brikker was challenged by the sentry, he stated that he had urgent business with Captain Carr and, after the customary formalities at the gate and at the Captain's quarters, he was admitted.

Although this was by no means the first time that Brikker had come to offer information, Carr was quite unprepared for the importance of what the Dutchman had brought on this occasion.

Brilliantly uniformed in scarlet and gold lace, bearing himself with the impressive dignity which befitted the representative of Governor Sir Francis Lovelace in the Delaware colonies, Carr received Hans Brikker in his office. His keen-featured ruddy countenance revealed his ability and power to deal effectively with situations as they arose.

He took the packet which Brikker laid on the table before him and unfastened the thong that bound it. Taking off the piece of deerskin that covered it, he lifted out three letters.

He broke the seals of these one after another and scanned the missives rapidly. Two were from Long Finn to Jan Stalcop and Juns Junstersen respectively. The other was from Armgart Printz to Stalcop. Long Finn's was not in his own hand, but it bore his mark.

Armgart's written by herself, though it betrayed that she knew what was on foot among the settlements, contained nothing to implicate her. It was cautious, ambiguous, non-committal throughout.

Long Finn's definitely incriminated him and those whom he addressed, proving beyond a shadow of doubt that they were guilty of plotting against His Britannic Majesty.

Carr looked up when he had perused the letters. "When did you get hold of these?" he inquired curtly of Brikker.

"Less than half an hour ago."

"How?"

"From an Indian, who had been told to take them to Stalcop and Junstersen."

"You paid the Indian for these?"

Hans Brikker grinned openly. "Certainly, respected sir, one does not get these things for nothing."

"How much?" Carr's piercing eyes searched the Dutchman's sly face.

That was a question that Brikker would not risk answering truthfully, therefore he lied. "When you have given me what you think is fair for bringing you these letters, respected sir, I will give him a present that will please him."

"Who is this Indian? His name?"

Brikker raised deprecating hands. "Do not ask me that, respected sir. He would not wish it known, even to you, who he is. I have sworn to keep it secret."

Carr lifted one shoulder indifferently. "Very well.

So that you bring me reliable information, I don't care where or how you get hold of it."

He rose from his chair, went to a small iron-bound chest in a corner of the room and, unlocking it, took out a bag of coins and counted out a small handful of gold.

The clinking of the money was music to Hans Brikker's ears. His greedy eyes told him that he was about to receive far more than he had expected.

Carr replaced the leathern bag, locked the chest, and returned to the table.

"This will pay you," he said, pouring the coins into Brikker's ready palm. "Keep on the lookout; get all you can from this Indian or anyone else. Lose no time in bringing it to me."

By this Hans Brikker understood that this time he must have furnished Carr with something of exceptional value. When he paused outside the fort in a spot where he could count his money unobserved, he was quite sure of it.

CHAPTER XVI

Nᴇᴡ Cᴀsᴛʟᴇ Mᴀʀᴋᴇᴛ
Plaine drowsed in the summer heat. Not a leaf on
the many trees which overshadowed it stirred in the
sultry air.

Hans Brikker in his shirt sleeves lolled outside his
door on Mink Street, puffing idly at his pipe. In the
kitchen Elsa was churning. For her there was no such
thing as rest during her waking hours. She had had
no beatings since the Orphan Master had forbidden

Brikker to strike her, but Brikker knew plenty of other methods of making her life miserable, and used them.

Two gentlemen, passing by the Dutchman's house, glanced casually at him. One was Philip Stanton, the other was Captain Carr.

"A brutal rascal," declared Stanton to his friend in an undertone.

"A useful man occasionally," affirmed Carr, thinking of the letters Brikker had obtained for him. These letters he would be sending to New York to Governor Lovelace shortly, but first he wished to discover more precisely how many and who among the Swedes and Finns were allied to Königsmarck.

He acquired this knowledge much sooner than he had anticipated, and in a way that he did not expect.

Secret invitations had been sent to every Swede and Finn along the Delaware to be guests of Long Finn that very evening at a supper in the house of a well-to-do Swede.

Those in sympathy with Long Finn's ideas were going, prepared to follow his lead in whatever he might propose. A number of others, of divided mind yet holding themselves open to conviction, meant to attend. Another group, loyal to the English, felt it incumbent upon them to be present in the hope that they might be able to sway the company in the right direction.

Lars Nilsson was invited with the rest. To the amazement of his wife and daughter, he announced that he was going.

"How is it possible!" exclaimed Ingeborg. "One would have supposed that you would stick your head in a nest of hornets sooner!"

She hung up a shirt which she had just finished ironing, and stared at him wide eyed.

"I should never have believed it," stammered Astrid, pausing in her task of scouring the wooden porridge bowls.

"My reason is good," asserted Lars. "Others, like myself, who are sure Long Finn is a rogue, feel that special mischief is on foot. They say it is their duty to be at this supper and prevent this mischief if they can. Peter Kock told me this. Besides, Gunnar will be there. I will use my authority to prevent his making a worse fool of himself than he has already."

No more was said. At the proper time, arrayed in his best clothes, Lars set out for the house where the supper was to be held. On the way to it, he met Eric Helm and his father, Anders.

"We must do what we can to show up this good-for-nothing, this Königsmarck, as he calls himself, for what he is," said Anders.

Lars nodded.

Peter Kock arrived at the door at the same moment as they. "We must keep our heads clear this evening," he declared. "There will be plenty of drink, and drunken men make fools of themselves."

"Trust me to keep sober," returned Lars.

"And us," promised Anders Helm for himself and his son.

The large room which they entered was crowded with men. The air was gray with the smoke from their pipes and reeked with the odor of the extra strong brandy used by the Swedes at such suppers and banquets. Thick strong beer stood about in casks.

Boards supported by trestles ran round the sides of the room and through the center of it. Great black pots and kettles of steaming food stood on the hearth or hung over the fire on iron cranes. Pork, venison, smoked fish, peas, beans, invited the hearty appetites of the guests.

There was a buzz of talk, and some who had already partaken freely of the brandy were beginning to argue noisily.

Long Finn moved from group to group, speaking a low word here, laying a friendly hand on someone's shoulder there; stirring this man or that to a stronger enthusiasm or more rooted faith in the outcome of the venture; trying to win to his cause those who hesitated or who opposed it altogether.

His tall lithe frame, with its alert virile strength, and the keenness of his strikingly handsome face conspired to make the more effective his natural magnetism.

For many weeks he had been sheltered and given refuge in Swedish homes as well as among the Indians. He had suffered no privations. Now the hour had struck, so he believed, for carrying out his ambitious schemes.

The moment Lars Nilsson had stepped into the room, he had looked around it expecting to see Gunnar among the company, but he was not there. Lars breathed a sigh of relief. Perhaps the lad had repented and drawn back at this crucial time. If only that were so!

He took an inconspicuous seat on a bench by the door. If Gunnar should come in, he would accost him at once.

Eric and Anders found places near him. Long Finn saw them, but for his own reasons did not approach them. They were glad of that.

Food was put upon the tables. The men drew up to the board close together on long benches and wooden stools but there was not room at the tables for everyone. Some had food offered to them wherever they were sitting. This was the case with Lars and Eric and Anders.

They had no desire to eat in a company of which Long Finn was one, but the host was an old acquaintance, and now that they had come to his house they could not refuse to break bread in it without giving serious offense.

Gunnar did not appear until the supper was begun. He entered in haste, flushed and exhilarated. His blue eyes sparkled and his lips were wreathed in a smile. He did not see his father, and was dashing past to get to some of his boon companions clustered about Evert Hindricksson.

An authoritative tap on his arm arrested him; a hand tightened on it. He looked down and saw Lars regarding him sternly.

Every trace of cheerful animation fled from Gunnar's face. Surprise and obstinacy replaced it. "You here?" he ejaculated. "How is that?"

"To see for myself what is going on. To help to put a stop to it. To bring you to your senses," replied Lars firmly.

Gunnar flung back his blond head. "I am with Long Finn to stay," he said flatly.

"And I am here to prevent you if you go too far tonight. Remember that you are not of age."

"That is something that you do not let me forget," retorted Gunnar, vibrating resentment and determined to pass on.

Lars released his son's arm without speaking.

Gunnar went directly to Hindrich Collmann and crowded into a seat beside him.

Anders and Eric had shrunk back a little while Lars was talking to Gunnar. It was not for them to push in at such a moment. They continued to keep silent. When Lars chose to address them, they would reply.

But he, too, remained silent, playing with his food, eating nothing, his burning eyes following his son's every movement.

Lusty appetites were finally sated, and drink began to circulate even freer than before.

Lars saw that Gunnar was taking far more liquor than he was used to. Several times he half rose to go to his son and try to check him, but changed his mind and sank to his seat again.

Long Finn, drinking sparingly, deliberately waited until most of the men were too befuddled by the strong brandy to realize the consequences of what they might do. Then, at what seemed to him an auspicious moment to inflame them, he rose.

"Men of New Sweden," he said in loud and resonant tones, "listen and be ready to act."

Every head was raised, every ear was roused to attention. Even the drunkest blinked, hiccoughed, and tried to understand.

Long Finn's great stature, the quality of his voice, made his words carry to the farthest corner of the big room.

"Men of New Sweden," he repeated, "the hour has come for you to shake off the yoke of your English oppressors. They have stolen from you one large piece of land after another. They have made you suffer, partly by fraud, partly by force. Free yourselves. Show yourselves men. Drive out these English. Have your own laws, your own ways. Have New Sweden again."

"The man has a tongue," murmured Lars to his companions, "but he is a rascal, nevertheless."

Gunnar leaned from his bench, his eyes glued to Long Finn, drinking in every syllable that he uttered. His cheeks burned, he thrilled from head to foot in the excess of his zeal.

Evert Hindricksson pounded his mug on the table. Men in every part of the room followed his example.

Peter Kock, Lars, Anders, Eric, and a handful of

others remained watchful and silent.

The silver tongue of Long Finn went on, exhorting, persuading, promising, arguing. "Outside the bay a fleet of warships from Sweden waits. These ships are full of armed men. They wait only for you to rise, to cast off your yoke, to sign allegiance to the King of Sweden. Do this. Fall upon the English. Slay them."

It could be seen that many were fully convinced. Long Finn went further. "Swear your allegiance to your rightful king, the King of Sweden. Speak now. Sign it now—tonight, this moment. I, Königsmarck, the king's messenger, call upon you to give your oath."

He held up a paper. Those who knew how to write their names upon it—well and good. Those who did not know how to handle a pen would have their names written for them, and would make their mark beside it.

Eager to be first to give allegiance, Gunnar leaped to his feet.

Lars Nilsson's voice, strong and stern, cut across the intervening space. "I forbid my son to give any such oath. He is not of age. He is a subject of England, as my oath made me for as long as my life lasts. He shall not swear—he shall not sign."

Gunnar glared furiously at his father.

Long Finn's steel-gray eyes sought and found Lars. He was about to answer him when suddenly Peter Kock jerked Gunnar down by the tail of his coat onto a bench, rose himself, and interrupted Long Finn before he was able to utter a word.

"It is true," he said, "that we are Swedes, and that these settlements were once New Sweden. But Sweden made no attempt to save us from the Dutch, nor from the English either. We Swedes, most of us, are honorable men. When we give an oath we stand to it. These lands were surrendered to the English years ago. An oath of allegiance to England for as long as our lives should last was required of us. We gave the oath, and as honorable men we should keep it."

A murmur ran around the room. Every ear was keyed for what Kock would say next, for it was obvious that he had not finished. He went on instantly.

"Do not listen to this man. There are no Swedish warships outside the bay. His name is not Königsmarck. He has not been sent from Sweden. He is an impostor, a cheat, who wishes to use you to further his own private schemes. Fellow Swedes—Finns, help me to arrest him."

Those in the room who had been stirred by Long Finn's appeal and were sober enough to think fairly straight, cast hurried glances at one another, uncertain as to what they should do. Those thoroughly drunk, scratched their heads, rubbed their foreheads, looked owlish, and drowsed off again.

Hindricksson, Collmann, Stalcop, clustered about Long Finn, prepared to contest Kock. Gunnar stepped forward with them.

But Long Finn did not hesitate, nor wait to be defended. He shoved aside to right and left the men around him and sprang for the door, intending to escape if he could. He alone knew the precise risks he would run by remaining. He would not stay and face them.

Though Long Finn was swift, Peter Kock was swifter. He was out of the door first, slammed it tight shut, and set his body against it.

The door opened outward. Long Finn hurled his weight upon it. It yielded by ever so little. He pushed harder with chest and shoulders.

Peter Kock on the outer side pushed with his own, opposing Long Finn with all his strength. While he pushed he shouted, demanding help to arrest Long Finn, help in preventing his escape.

The men in the room sat or stood as if under a

spell. None except Lars, Anders and Eric responded. They tried to haul him back, to hold him.

Long Finn was very tall and powerful, and using his arms like flails, he beat them off. By a mighty lunge of his body he forced the door open a couple of inches, thrust his hand through and held the edge of the door to prevent its closing.

Peter Kock snatched out his knife and hacked at Long Finn's fingers with the sharp blade. The knife cut deep and blood flowed freely.

Long Finn pressed his teeth together, repressing a cry of pain. Fury made him stronger. One final tremendous effort on his part and the door gave way for him. Peter Kock was knocked off his feet and out of the path, and Long Finn bolted off into the blackness of the night.

Hotfoot along with him sped Hindrich Collmann and Gunnar.

CHAPTER XVII

THE ESCAPE OF LONG Finn was succeeded instantly by an uproar in the crowded room. Drunken men, staggering to their feet, stumbled over stools and benches. Several fell headlong to the floor.

The men who were sober, or partly sober, elbowed and pushed themselves free of the confusion. There was a babel of shouts, curses, voices raised in protest or in heated argument. Adherents of Long Finn tried to start quarrels and fights with those who opposed them. Knives came out.

The wiser and more cautious began to slip out of the door and away to their homes. First to leave the place were Lars and his companions. Long Finn had only just fled, and Peter Kock was trying to regain his balance.

Eric put out an arm to help him.

Kock took him by the shoulder and shook it to emphasize his words. "You have young swift legs, Eric. Use them. Run as fast as you can to the fort. Tell the officer there to send soldiers to catch Long Finn and arrest him; to arrest the men, too, who are in the plot with him. I'll go to Captain Carr myself. But you can outstrip me, and there is not a minute to be lost. Make speed."

Eric needed no urging. He was off like a shot.

Peter Kock followed as rapidly as he could in the same direction, but Eric was soon far ahead of him.

Lars and Anders moved slowly through the darkness.

"If only my boy had the sense of yours," muttered Lars to his old friend.

"Eric is a good lad," agreed Anders. "But do not take this too hard, Lars. Your son has been led astray from the right track by the tongue of this Long Finn, it is true. That is no sign, however, that he will not return to it, that you may not yet be proud of him."

Lars shook his head dolefully. Nothing seemed more unlikely to him.

Although he doubted the reclaiming of his son, neither Astrid nor her mother could give up hope for Gunnar.

When Lars left them to go to the supper, they had their own simple meal and attended to the household chores. The twins were tucked in for the night earlier than usual.

An unwonted quiet settled over the kitchen. Neither Lars, smoking his evening pipe on the long bench, nor Gunnar, laughing, joking, arguing, grumbling, was there to start talk and keep it going.

Lars would return in a few hours at the utmost. But Gunnar? That was a question that no one could answer.

Ingeborg got out her bread trough, measured flour, salt and fat, and poured in home-made yeast and water. She mixed and kneaded all together for the night's rising and tomorrow's baking. Astrid went to the garden to weed her beds for she had been obliged to neglect them lately.

The girl was restless in body and spirit. This work among the flowers might soothe and steady her.

Kneading the mass of dough might do the same for her mother.

However, they were unable to detach their thoughts from Lars and Gunnar. Their imaginations revolved around those two, together in the flesh in the room where Long Finn's supper was in progress, yet far apart as the poles in aims and ideas. What would the outcome of this evening be for them both?

Ingeborg's brows knit painfully as she asked it of herself while she kneaded the dough mechanically.

Astrid pondered it, her eyes dim as she plucked up every intruding weed and stirred the earth about the roots of her favorite plants.

Darkness overtook them. Ingeborg finished her task; Astrid forsook hers. With one accord they went to the long bench outside the door, and sat down side by side upon it. Each clasped her hands tightly in her lap.

In a tense unbroken silence they remained so, only shifting the position of their bodies a little now and then.

An hour, two hours, they sat thus. Lars ought to be back soon now, they thought to themselves. He would not stay at the supper longer than necessary to make sure of what Gunnar would do.

All at once they saw Eric running as if for dear

life toward Fort Casimir. He did not so much as turn his head in their direction to give them greeting. They wondered at that.

Ten minutes later a detail of soldiers from the fort marched by and up the Tinicum Road.

"There must be trouble somewhere," murmured Ingeborg through dry lips.

"At the supper," guessed Astrid huskily.

Back marched the soldiers before a great while, herding men drunk and men sober to the fort. There was no sign of Long Finn among the prisoners. Lars was not among them either, nor was Gunnar.

Astrid and her mother breathed more freely because of this.

Not for long.

A few minutes later Lars and Anders emerged from a secluded footpath well to the right of the road. They came on together to the garden gate and paused there to say good night to one another.

"Thank God they are safe," whispered Ingeborg, pressing Astrid's arm convulsively.

She had no more than said it when four soldiers seemed to leap out of the earth and seized Lars and Anders.

"Two more of the scoundrels," barked the corporal in command. "March 'em along."

Lars tried to release himself, protesting his innocence of any wrong-doing. Anders did the same.

"You were at the supper," replied the corporal, in cold disbelief. "That means that you were up to mischief, the same as the rest."

Ingeborg and Astrid had sprung up; they flew to the gate and out of it.

Lars was endeavoring to explain to the corporal. The corporal refused to listen.

"What he says is true," cried Astrid in an agony of pleading. "He went to persuade others not to link themselves to the Long Finn—for that and nothing else."

"He speaks the truth—the truth," protested Ingeborg over her clasped hands.

"He can tell that at the fort when he is questioned there," returned the corporal stiffly. "For the present he goes to jail with the rest."

Without more ado the two guiltless men were marched off between the soldiers.

"Do not be troubled, Ingeborg. Do not be troubled, Astrid," called Lars as he was being led away. "I shall be cleared soon enough. Peter Kock knows, everyone knows, that I have been against Long Finn from the beginning."

Such unshakable confidence rang in his tones that

his wife and daughter were heartened in spite of their fears.

"Hindrich Collmann can vouch for him, and plenty of others can do the same, if they will," averred Astrid, bolstering up her mother's courage and her own.

The more they thought it over, the simpler and easier it appeared that Lars would shortly be restored to liberty.

In this they reckoned without Hans Brikker.

He was having his tankard of ale in the tavern that evening when townsfolk commenced to stream in bringing excited rumors of the supper and what had gone on there.

An incontestable fact out of the mass of conflicting rumors was that soldiers sent from the fort had rounded up a good many of those present at the supper, and that Lars Nilsson had been taken into custody, although his son Gunnar had escaped.

No guilt could be ascribed to Lars, as Brikker knew very well, but he knew equally well that Gunnar was an open and enthusiastic follower of the man who called himself Königsmarck.

Lars had attended the supper. Therefore it would sound plausible to accuse him of being secretly in favor of Königsmarck though outwardly he had pre-

[183]

tended out of prudence to oppose the plot for an uprising.

Brikker drained his tankard and left the taproom.

The hour was not late. He might be so fortunate as to get speech with Captain Carr that night.

He was not disappointed. Carr was still in his office. He had already received the report of his subordinate officer concerning the arrests made, an important addition to the letters of Long Finn and Armgart Printz which had been furnished him by Brikker.

As soon as he had obtained the sworn testimony of several reliable persons who had witnessed what had happened at the supper, he would send the whole report to Governor Lovelace with an explanatory letter.

He was perfectly willing to hear what Hans Brikker might have to say in regard to certain of these witnesses. Peter Kock had already assured him as to the loyalty and good faith of Lars Nilsson and Anders Helm. Eric Helm, who had brought Kock's message before Kock himself was able to arrive, was naturally above suspicion. Carr's surprise was considerable, therefore, when Hans Brikker appeared and made his accusation.

"What you say," he told the Dutchman, "does

not agree with what I hear from others about Lars Nilsson. By all accounts he is a good and honest man."

"It would not be the first time, respected sir," suggested Brikker, rubbing his palms together, "that people have been deceived in a man."

This being obvious, Carr did not trouble to reply to it. He was not at all convinced that Brikker was everything that he pretended to be, but he was an excellent intelligence gatherer, which was all that he required of him.

"Nilsson's son is loose," Brikker went on to remind him. "He is a fiery young fellow, up to every kind of mischief—one of the worst."

"Find out where he is, if you can," Carr instructed him. "But whoever else escapes, we must not fail to capture Long Finn."

Brikker was obliged to depart without having learned whether Lars Nilsson was to remain a prisoner for any lengthy period.

Captain Carr debated this point in his own mind when he was left alone. His final decision was that it would be wise to keep Lars in confinement until Gunnar was captured or came voluntarily out of hiding and gave himself up.

Astrid and her mother lay awake the night

through, praying that Lars and Gunnar might be restored to them.

Eric made haste to them in the morning, and broke the news of what they must expect. Anders had been released. Peter Kock was using his influence for Lars, but thus far in vain.

Ingeborg covered her face, stricken dumb by so much misfortune.

Astrid lifted her head high. Her eyes met Eric's with a flash like steel. "Gunnar must be found," she said. "He must come home and bear the punishment for his wrongdoing himself."

CHAPTER XVIII

JUFFROU PRINTZ, THE "proud lady of Tinicum," kept herself secluded in her own house while soldiers scoured the country round for Long Finn. She was careful to display no special interest in the matter, nor betray any more than ordinary knowledge of him and his plight.

Only old Olga could say positively that he had ever darkened the doors of Printz Torp. Only Olga could bear witness that he had been a frequent visitor there, though always in secret and by night.

That was all that Olga knew, and Olga could and would hold her tongue. Armgart would deny connivance with his schemes if she were brought before a judge, and if it were discovered that she had ever talked with him, she would protest that he had sought her without result. So far as she knew, not a shred of proof existed that it had been otherwise.

From Olle she had heard the story, which he had obtained from others, of Long Finn's flight. She did not know where he was now, nor what would become of him, nor did she care. He had failed and she was through with him. A chance to increase her private fortune and gratification of her personal ambitions had been all that had induced her to have any dealings with him; these had been the motives of her acts.

Long Finn, if he were caught and brought to trial, might try to implicate her, and she, too, might be tried, but his unsupported evidence alone would not suffice to convict her.

There was strong probability that he had made good his escape, that he would never return nor make a second attempt to stir up revolt.

She had never felt entire confidence in his claims. Now she doubted them altogether.

Most of the prisoners taken on the night of Long Finn's supper had been released from Fort Casimir on the following day. Those who were guiltless, and had accepted the supper invitation merely to exert a good influence if matters came to a head, were exonerated. Those who had been led astray foolishly were liberated with the understanding that they must present themselves in answer to summons when instructions concerning them were received by Captain Carr from Governor Lovelace.

Several of the chief offenders and fomenters of the plot were kept in close confinement.

Although Peter Kock did everything he could to gain the release of Lars Nilsson, and repeated to Captain Carr the very words that Lars had spoken to his son at the supper, to which others bore witness also, Carr made it public that he was holding Lars as hostage for Gunnar and that he would not set him free until Gunnar came to take his place as the guilty one.

There was a warrant out for the arrest of Hindrich Collmann, and proclamation was made that if he did not surrender himself to Carr within fifteen days, his entire estate would be seized and confiscated to the Crown.

These were sad days for Astrid and her mother.

Officers of the law were searching diligently for Gunnar to bring him to punishment. Lars was suffering for his sake.

"If Gunnar could only know that father is kept in jail on his account he would come back quickly," affirmed Astrid.

"That he would," agreed Ingeborg.

They were in the cornfield, cutting the ripe corn. The hot sun poured upon them as they moved along the rows, leaving behind them on the ground heaps of corn in the husk.

Now and then they paused to wipe the sweat from their faces with their aprons. The glistening leaves of the tall plants rustled crisply as the two brushed against them.

Karin and Kirsten played at hide and seek between the rows of jointed stalks.

Sultry air, rapidly massing clouds, promised a thunderstorm.

"Eric is trying his best to find out what has become of Gunnar," continued Astrid.

"Gunnar has probably hidden himself among the savages beyond Tinicum," returned Ingeborg despondently. "Never would we have believed that our Gunnar, so dutiful and obedient as a child and growing boy, would cause us such sorrow and anxiety since he has become almost a man."

To this Astrid made no reply, for a sudden splashing of raindrops upon the corn blades and the loud roll of thunder, made them both forsake corn cutting, snatch up the twins, and speed to the shelter of the house.

Lars in his dingy cell at Fort Casimir was as despondent as his family. Added to the disgrace which Gunnar had brought upon them all, the confinement and idleness, instead of his accustomed active life of physical labor, told upon him. There was also the acute concern which he felt for his family in the work about the farm at this time of harvesting, and the provision for his wife and children during the winter months.

Above and beyond all were the anxieties aroused in him by rumors of ruinous fines and taking away of property from offenders against the government. He was guiltless to be sure, but he might have to pay a large fine, if nothing more, on Gunnar's account. This he could by no means afford.

During his lonely hours in prison he struggled against the bitter resentment toward his son which surged within him, but these struggles were not crowned with success.

"Obstinate, foolish, if he had only listened to me,

none of this would have happened," he complained to himself, sitting solitary on a rickety wooden stool in his bare cell, his hands pressed to his forehead, his eyes dark with gloom.

A number of days elapsed. Hans Brikker strutted about New Castle vastly pleased over the misfortunes which had overtaken the Nilssons. He considered that his old scores were being paid off handsomely.

He kept on the lookout for Running Weasel, hoping to discover through him the whereabouts of Long Finn. He was convinced that the man was somewhere among the Indians, taking refuge there until he could travel still farther away without risk of being captured.

His surmise was correct. Running Weasel presented himself one evening outside the tavern door to verify it.

Brikker supplied himself with the expected flask of brandy and repaired to the customary rendezvous.

"If my brother wishes to catch the Long Finn, let the soldiers come and take him. Running Weasel knows the place where he stays," the savage informed him, his black eyes glittering in anticipation of the "firewater" which the Dutchman was to give him.

"You will go with the soldiers and show them exactly where he is?" inquired Brikker.

Running Weasel bent his shaven head in assent.

"When?" asked Brikker.

"Now," replied Running Weasel.

"Go to the fort and wait outside the gate," Brikker instructed him. "I will go in and speak to the officer. The soldiers will march out and follow you to where Long Finn hides."

"Firewater first," demanded Running Weasel.

"Not first," returned Brikker firmly. "After Long Finn is caught, then plenty."

Running Weasel scowled and protested.

Brikker held his ground. "After Long Finn is caught, then plenty," he repeated.

The Indian was obliged to yield. "Then plenty— plenty much," he stipulated, to make sure of his bargain.

"Plenty much," Brikker promised him.

As if in warning, Running Weasel drew his scalping knife from his belt and ran his fingers along its blade significantly.

Brikker understood. "Plenty much," he repeated quickly, "plenty much."

The thirsty savage grunted. "Running Weasel himself shall say how much."

Hans Brikker let the matter rest there.

Together they went to Fort Casimir. Brikker

gained admittance at the sally-port. Running Weasel waited outside.

Within the quarter-hour a file of soldiers was stepping quietly along a forest trail following a naked red man who was their guide.

Hans Brikker was not with them. He had done his part by supplying the information to Captain Carr. He was to be rewarded abundantly for it when Long Finn was securely lodged behind prison bars. After that he had to satisfy Running Weasel, but he did not expect that to be too difficult.

Next morning New Castle awoke to hear that Long Finn had been caught; that he was already imprisoned in the fort; that an Indian had led soldiers to his hiding place and they had taken him unawares.

Astrid, who had risen in the gray light of early morning to milk the cow, was returning to the house with a brimming bucket when the soldiers marched into New Castle with their captive by way of the Tinicum Road.

She saw them from a distance but that did not prevent her instant recognition of Long Finn.

He walked tall and straight with a swinging stride, his handsome head held insolently, his shoulders squared.

Captors and captive passed on to the fort.

Astrid hurried to the house, set down her bucket upon the table, and sank onto the nearest bench.

Her knees were suddenly limp.

"They have caught Long Finn," she cried, quivering from head to foot in her excitement.

Ingeborg whirled toward her from the hearth where she had been putting corn bread to bake in the hot ashes.

"But not Gunnar?" she asked low.

"No, not Gunnar," returned Astrid.

CHAPTER XIX

The anvil of Barnard the smith rang under the mighty blows of his hammer falling on red-hot iron. He was forging strong chains for Long Finn.

These were urgently required and must be completed as soon as possible, for Long Finn had tried to escape and had almost succeeded.

New Castle was having its fill of surprises in relation to Long Finn. He had been confronted with

Peter Kock by Captain Carr. Kock had said to him, "You rascal, tell me, what is your name? For we can see well that you are no honorable person."

Long Finn had flung out sullenly that his true name was Marcus Jacobson, and had admitted that he had no right whatever to the name of Königsmarck.

That was not all. It was discovered that he had gone by other names in other places. Among his aliases were those of John Binckson and Matthew Hinks. Born a Swede, he had gone to England. There he had committed some criminal offense and, because of it, had been transported to Maryland, and sold as a slave to serve in that colony for a term of years.

Burning with hatred of the English, determined on revenge, he had managed to escape from his master in Maryland and make his way to New Castle. As an adventurer under the pretended name of Königsmarck, he had imposed upon his unsuspecting countrymen in the settlements on the Delaware, hoping by means of them to stir up trouble for the English.

Armgart Printz congratulated herself now more than ever that she had not allowed herself to be caught up inextricably into his schemes. Safe in Printz Torp, she kept sharp track of the course of events connected with him, and of the persons whom he had involved. She continued to give no outward sign that she took any interest in his or their fate, beyond what might reasonably be expected of any dweller in the settlements.

Those of her countrymen who knew or suspected that she had secretly abetted and encouraged Long Finn in what he had attempted, held their peace. She was a Swede and a woman, and they would let her keep her skirts clear if she could.

Hans Brikker, not satisfied with the fact that Lars was in prison and Gunnar a fugitive, was determined to have Gunnar brought to punishment. He counted upon Running Weasel's assistance in this.

Thus far the Minqua had not been able to locate him. In the meantime he had become more persistent and threatening in his demands for "firewater." Brikker had difficulty in holding him off. He could only do it at all by promising him an abundance when he had found Gunnar.

None knew better than Gunnar the coverts and hiding places that might afford him secure shelter. The fertile lands, the high bold shore, the creeks, the caves, the forests and swamps along the blue and sparkling Delaware, from above Tinicum to below New Castle, were familiar to him from earliest boyhood. He had hunted and fished the length and breadth of them at all seasons of the year. Among them he could lose himself indefinitely.

Eric Helm, as well as Hans Brikker, was bent upon finding Gunnar for he was as confident as Astrid that if Gunnar could only be told of what had happened to his father, he would hurry to New Castle of his own accord and offer himself up. If he could learn how false Long Finn's claims and assertions had been, he would be bitterly ashamed that he had ever listened to him, had ever followed him.

The problem for Eric was how to get this news to him. Anders was busy with the fishing and could ill afford to do without his son's help. Eric longed to aid Astrid, Lars and Ingeborg, and Gunnar, too, by recalling him to his responsibilities. He could understand and foresee what agony of soul Gunnar would experience later if he failed the ones who loved him in this crisis.

Anders and he were hauling in their nets on a sunny morning. Eric's face was grave and downcast.

The net was brought over the gunwale of the boat, the flopping glistening fish secured. Anders let them lie and fastened a searching gaze upon his son.

"Something troubles you, Eric. Out with it."

Eric hesitated to admit it. His father needed him.

"Out with it, my boy. We have no secrets from one another. We do not forget our friends either. What is it that you want to do?"

"To find Gunnar," confessed Eric, "and to tell him what has happened. He has not heard or he would have shown himself long since. He would never let someone else bear punishment that he should bear."

"No, never," agreed Anders. "Go, then, Eric. Look for him. You know better than anyone else where he is likely to be. Stay away as long as necessary. I can manage. In that way, I, too, will be doing a little to assist my old friends."

Before midday Eric stopped at Lars Nilsson's door to let Astrid and Ingeborg know where he was going. He had his musket, powder horn, bullet pouch and hunting-knife. A small sack of provisions was strapped to his shoulders.

"I may be gone for some time; I may return soon. However that may be, I shall bring news of Gunnar when I come."

"Go, and God bless you," said Ingeborg fervently, and kissed him on both cheeks. Her eyes were blurred; her voice shook.

"Go, and God bless you," repeated Astrid solemnly. "Day and night we will pray that you will be guided to him. We know well what will happen if you do."

Eric did not expect the task he had set for himself would be easy. Nor was it.

Obviously Gunnar had not resorted for refuge to such places as he had been most apt to frequent in the past. Neither had he gone, as Long Finn and Collmann had done, to friendly Indians. Soldiers, officers of the law, had already sought him there in vain.

Eric scoured far and wide, overlooking no hidden cove or inlet nor the woods that bordered them, no lonely creek nor brook that wound away through dense forests. Oftentimes he came upon the ashes of a dead campfire, but these might have been left by any traveler journeying that way.

Several days passed in fruitless quest. One afternoon he arrived at the brink of a creek beyond Tinicum which wound far to the north. Traders used the creek and the trail that ran near it, but to Eric's knowledge Gunnar had never gone along either.

He was tired and sat down on a mossy bank to consider the situation. On the whole it did not appear to him probable that Gunnar would believe the Long

Finn's cause was altogether lost; he would suppose that Long Finn and Hindrich Collmann were somewhere in hiding. Therefore, unless he heard to the contrary, he would hold himself in readiness to rejoin them at a favorable opportunity. In order to do this he must remain in the vicinity of their old haunts, so this side of the creek would naturally be the boundary to his wanderings.

Eric supposed that he had investigated every nook and corner that could give shelter to Gunnar. To be sure, he just might have missed him at any point. Or Gunnar might have seen him again and again and purposely eluded him.

Therefore he must go over the entire ground once more in the hope that he might have better success this time, might stumble upon him most unexpectedly. He would not allow himself to be defeated nor discouraged.

He was spared the trouble of further search. A figure that had been slipping behind him hesitantly for the past half hour, using tree trunks as cover to his movements, was at the moment concealed by the bole of a giant beech a couple of yards from where Eric sat, his musket across his knees. Apparently he could not decide whether or not to show himself.

But when he saw Eric rise as if to go on, he flung

hesitation aside, sprang out, and stirred by sudden impulse, reached him at a bound.

"Eric! Stop!" he cried.

Startled by the familiar unexpected voice, Eric swung round. "Gunnar!" he exclaimed.

"What news from home?" demanded Gunnar eagerly.

Eric dealt him the first blow. "Long Finn is in prison. He has turned out to be what some of us supposed him to be all along—an impostor."

Gunnar flushed angrily. "He is not an impostor. He came to free us."

"You are mistaken. He has confessed that he has no right to the name of Königsmarck. He is a common fellow; was a criminal in England; was sent as a convict slave to Maryland; escaped from his master to us Swedes on the Delaware to make trouble for the English because he hates them. All this has been found out."

Gunnar looked at him blankly, stunned by these revelations. "But—but—" he stammered, and then choked.

"He admits the truth of what I have told you," continued Eric. "Those who did most to support him, Jan Stalcop and a few others, are in jail too, in chains like himself. Hindrich Collmann is there. He was given fifteen days to present himself to Captain Carr, unless he wished to lose all his property; so he came when he learned that Long Finn had deceived him."

Gunnar was speechless with dismay.

Eric saw that the moment had come when he must receive the second blow.

"Your father is in jail also," he informed him gravely.

"My father!" shouted Gunnar in amaze. "Why?"

"Instead of you. They mean to hold him until you come and give yourself up. What punishment you may have to bear I do not know. But in the mean.time your father is punished for you by being kept in jail. It goes hard with him and with your family."

"My father shall not stay in jail on my account," rapped out Gunnar, turning on his heel. "I am going instantly to free him and take my punishment myself."

He was already several yards away, forging ahead in furious haste when Eric overtook him, saying, "I was sure you would go at once, Gunnar, as soon as you knew. That is why I came to look for you."

"What else?" returned Gunnar, throwing him a sidewise glance.

"Astrid was sure, too," said Eric, keeping brisk step with him.

"Astrid understands me," murmured Gunnar.

They traveled the Tinicum Road, leaving the miles behind them with incredible celerity. Even so, Gunnar's long legs could not keep pace with the urging of his spirit. Remorse welled up in him, a veritable agony of penitence, and a desire to make what amends he could for his rebellious past.

They had approached to within a rod of Lars Nilsson's house when Gunnar halted abruptly. His home still was hidden from him by a slight bend in the road.

"I must go in, if only for an instant, to speak to my mother and Astrid, to let them know that I have come." He brought forth the words painfully.

Eric guessed his feeling. "Yes, you must," he replied. He dropped back so that Gunnar might go on alone to his family. It was never his way to intrude.

The house door was wide open when Gunnar arrived at the threshold. Ingeborg was sifting meal slowly into a pot of boiling water for the evening porridge. Astrid was washing the hands and faces of the twins.

Gunnar looked in hungrily, his foot on the sill.

Kirsten spied him. "Gunnar!" she shrieked. "My

Gunnar!" She broke from Astrid and rushed to him to grasp him round the knees.

Karin ran too. "Gunnar! My Gunnar!" she echoed.

The meal in Ingeborg's hand plopped into the water in a lump. Astrid cast away in a wet mass the cloth with which she had been wiping Karin's cheeks.

Immediately Gunnar was drawn in, surrounded.

He laid a tender hand for a second on the flaxen heads of the little ones. Then he lifted his eyes to Ingeborg's. "Mother," he whispered. Caught into that single word were his acute remorse, his penitence, his grief.

"Gunnar!" sobbed Ingeborg, and speaking his name and no more she poured into it her love, her forgiveness.

Her arms went round him. He bowed his head upon her breast and held her to him.

Astrid touched his head affectionately. "Dear Gunnar, our Gunnar," she breathed.

He did not tarry, nor did they ask him to do so. He must go at once and fulfill the purpose of his return.

Eric went with him to the fort gate but parted from him there. "God will be with you, Gunnar," he said, wringing his friend's hand.

The cell in which Lars was confined was almost dark in the fading light when Gunnar was conducted to it by the guard.

Lars glanced up inquiringly from his bench when the key grated in the lock. This was not the hour for his evening meal. So far as he was aware there could be no other reason why anyone would break in upon his wretched solitude.

The gloom and depression natural to a Swede under misfortune were gaining a stronger and stronger hold upon him. How long must he stay in this hateful inaction?

His question had swift answer. The door opened and Gunnar was at his knees, clasping them, his head upon them, gulping out wild prayers for forgiveness.

Lars raised Gunnar's head between his toilworn hands. His clear blue eyes looked deep into his son's. "Say no more, my boy," he bade him. "You have come home, and to your senses."

"That you have been here—here in prison for my sake," began Gunnar.

His father checked him. "Say no more, my son," he repeated affectionately, "say no more. Let the past rest."

Lars went forth from the prison a free man.

The door of the cell clanged shut upon Gunnar. He was there to await his sentence, whatever that might be, but from his heart turbulence and rebellion had departed.

CHAPTER XX

Long Finn was to be tried on December sixth in the Court Room in Fort Casimir.

A Commission, headed by Mr. Matthias Nicoll as president, had been sent by Governor Lovelace from New York on November twenty-second to conduct the trial according to law.

Excitement ran high in New Castle, for those who

had taken part in the plot were to be sentenced at the same time as Long Finn. Those not in prison were summoned to appear at the trial.

Governor Lovelace had sent specific instructions to Captain Carr as to how Long Finn and his accomplices were to be punished, but left him to use his own judgment as to the severity to be exercised in the cases of milder offenders.

Under which of these heads Gunnar would be classed was a source of the greatest concern to his parents and to Astrid. He was so young, had been led away by the persuasive tongues of Long Finn and Hindrich Collmann. On the other hand he had been much with Evert Hindricksson. That would tell against him.

Eric Helm offered Astrid what hope and encouragement he honestly could, but that was not much for he had grave doubts about the issue. It would be better for her not to set her hopes too high in the beginning, only to have them dashed to pieces later.

Never had such silence prevailed in Astrid's home as during those days of suspense. She and her mother performed their household tasks mechanically, rarely speaking. Karin and Kirsten in happy childish ignorance were as merry and playful as ever. Lars, now that work in the fields was over for the season, spent his time in going over his farm implements, putting them in order, and in making repairs in and around the house and outbuildings. He was as silent as his wife and eldest daughter.

Prayers for Gunnar, often unspoken but fervent, rose daily from the hearts of the three. He was so young; he had been so obstinate and foolish, yet there was good, much good in him. They could not bear to have his life broken on the very threshold of his manhood.

One day before the trial, Astrid's despondent accents cut across the brooding silence. "Is there no one who could speak a good word for our Gunnar?"

It was in the middle of the afternoon when she addressed her father thus.

Lars was busy at his workbench at the farther end of the kitchen. He glanced up from a large wooden trough which he was shaping. His tone, his look in answering were as despondent as his daughter's.

"I can think of no one. In former days Hindrich Collmann is the man to whom I would have turned in a case like this. He would have had influence then. But as we know, he is one of the worst transgressors. He will have to pay a heavy price for that, and can do nothing for others."

He bent his head over his work again.

Ingeborg had listened intently to his reply. It offered no ray of encouragement. She drooped her own head and drove her needle in and out rapidly through the cloth of a new bodice she was fashioning for Karin, but she could hardly see her stitches because of the tears in her eyes.

Astrid threw down her knitting, hurried to the peg by the door where her cloak and hood hung. She put the garments on. "I must go out into the air," she said huskily.

She went out and closed the door tightly behind her. It was impossible for her to endure the gloom that hovered in the kitchen any longer.

Early snow powdered the ground. The purity and crispness of the air, and its coldness, braced her for a little.

As though by the swiftness of her steps she might find brief release from her fears for Gunnar which were consuming her, she fled toward the solitude of the borders of the Bouwerie Wood.

She did not get quite that far. Philip Stanton, advancing along a trail that emerged abruptly from the wood, saw her and quickened his footsteps. He knew that Gunnar was in prison awaiting trial and he could

*Philip Stanton went directly to the point. "You are afraid for
your brother."*

guess how troubled this girl was as to her brother's fate.

Stanton had no idea that he would be able to help her in the unhappy situation, but he thought a kindly word might not come amiss.

"A fine winter day," he said cheerily, confronting her. He noted how clouded her eyes were, how strained the expression of her face.

"Yes," replied Astrid somberly, "I suppose it is." The frigid beauty of the wintry day could not lift the weight that crushed her spirit, nor make her forget her fears for Gunnar.

Philip Stanton went directly to the point. "You are afraid for your brother."

"Yes, for Gunnar," she admitted sadly, pulling her cloak closer round her. They were standing still where they had met, upon the open road outside the wood, and there was a sharp sting to the air.

"Do not forget this," Stanton told her, in an effort to revive her fainting courage, "your brother is very young, and for that reason if for no other, the judges may be lenient toward him."

"That is my only hope, my parents' only hope," returned Astrid in smothered tones.

"If I have any power to help him, be sure I will use it," said Stanton earnestly.

Astrid could not imagine what power so young a man could have in such an emergency, nor how he could succeed in swaying judges.

Nor did Stanton know, but there was a man whom he could and would approach who would have considerable influence, if not absolute authority, in the pronouncement of the verdict.

He made it his business that evening to take up the subject with Captain Carr, whose guest he was at dinner.

"The poor fellow is so young," he pleaded over the nut that he was cracking.

The meal was over and Carr was sipping his Madeira appreciatively. "Not too young," he returned, "to get himself mixed up with that desperado, Evert Hindricksson. He was unwise in choosing his companions."

"That was because of Long Finn," Stanton reminded him promptly. "If mercy be shown to Gunnar Nilsson he may turn out to be as good and loyal a citizen as his father, Lars."

Carr smiled away his companion's arguments one after another as Stanton continued to plead Gunnar's cause. He gave him no satisfaction whatever.

"The trial is tomorrow," he said finally. "His case will be decided then."

As many of the inhabitants of New Castle as could crowd into the Court Room were there next day to witness the trial and hear the verdicts. At that time New Castle Court House was not yet built. A room on the second floor of the fort was used as a Court Room, and Governor Lovelace had sent orders to Captain Carr that Long Finn was to be tried there.

In the fort enclosure behind the fort walls a mass of people were clustered in groups. These were from all the settlements along the Delaware River.

The Commission sent by Lovelace occupied the judges' seats. They wore no official robes. Broadcloth, satin, velvet, in bright or somber hues, clothed them. Lace drooped from about their wrists and cascaded over their brocaded waistcoats. They bore themselves with solemn dignity, as befitted those who were to administer justice.

Astrid and her parents had managed to squeeze in at the back of the Court Room. There being no one with whom the twins could be left, Ingeborg gripped Karin tightly by the hand, and Lars kept firm hold of Kirsten.

In sickening dread the three elders stood waiting, wondering miserably what Gunnar's fate was to be. Their trembling hopes had faded utterly. Almost breath and life seemed suspended in the intensity of these hours of dreadful waiting.

All at once the voice of the court crier was raised. "Silence is commanded in the court whilst His Majesty's Commission is sitting, on pain of imprisonment."

Instantly the subdued hum of talk among the people ceased. Dead silence prevailed in the Court Room. Every eye was fixed on the gentlemen of the Commission. Every ear was keyed to catch the words that would issue from their lips.

The names of the Commission were called. Proclamation was made that witnesses should draw near. A jury of twelve men was empaneled.

These preliminaries completed, Long Finn was brought from prison to stand before his judges.

Astrid and the others in the Court Room heard the clanking of his chains as he was marched up the stair and to the bar.

He passed within a foot of Astrid when he was marshaled through the door. His head was raised as high as ever it had been. His eyes burned with a smoldering hate and resentment. No mar was on his handsome face as yet. None in that assemblage stood so tall and aggressively bold as he. A magnetic quality was in his face and features which made it easy to understand how he had contrived to draw to him the credulous and the simple-hearted.

A few more formal preliminaries, the jury sworn and bid to look upon the prisoner, and then the command to Long Finn under his own name and his aliases:

"Marcus Jacobson, John Binkson, Matthew Hinks, hold up your right hand."

He obeyed and was accused, witnesses were called and testimony given. The prisoner was allowed to speak for himself if he chose. The jury received its charge from the Commission, withdrew to the jury room, and returned thence with a verdict of "Guilty."

Long Finn stood like a stone while his sentence was read. He had been adjudged worthy of death by the Council in New York, but they decided upon a sentence more terrible than death itself. He was to be publicly and severely whipped; the letter R for rebel was to be branded on his face; a large inscription stating his crime was to be written and fastened to his breast; and after all these, he was to be sent in chains to New York, and from thence to Barbadoes to be sold as a slave to serve for four years, or longer, as might be customary in that place.

He was taken back to his cell. Again his chains clanked and rattled as he went.

Astrid, looking up at him, knew that it would be the last day on which his countenance would be seen unmarred. Henceforth the world was to know his guilt at a glance. There would be no hiding it.

The horror of such a fate could hardly be Gunnar's, and yet it might be that his sentence would be severe enough to crush him and those who loved him to the earth.

Orders were given to bring in the other offenders who were imprisoned. That would include Gunnar.

Every muscle in Lars' face tightened. A deathly pallor overspread Ingeborg's naturally ruddy skin. Astrid clenched her hands and held them one upon another at her breast. A stifling terror took her by the throat.

Jan Stalcop and the other chief offenders were brought in in chains. Evert Hindricksson also, rough and reckless as ever in his bearing. Gunnar, subdued and repentant, came last. Others not imprisoned, but who had been summoned, followed after.

They were ranged before the bar and their sentences pronounced. For these there was to be no flogging, no slavery, but some were to receive the brand ("the mark" as it was called). Enormous fines that would keep these chief offenders and their families impoverished for years and confiscation of half their properties were to be the punishments. The amounts of the individual fines were left entirely to Captain Carr's discretion. Lesser offenders were to pay smaller fines.

The "proud lady of Tinicum" had not been brought to trial. No proof against her had been discovered; no witnesses spoke in her disfavor. Therefore she was absolved of guilt.

She had not shown herself in the Court Room, maintaining consistently her assumed indifference as to what might take place at the trial.

At her house at Printz Torp, nevertheless, she was having qualms, for she felt by no means certain that one or other of the witnesses or the guilty parties might not say something that would turn searching inquiry in her direction.

Long Finn had sworn not to betray her, but he had been exposed as an utter rascal and an impostor, and she did not trust him now in any particular.

She need not have been troubled. Lord Lovelace had written to Captain Carr that after having read her intercepted letter which Carr had forwarded to him, he was convinced that while she had doubtless sympathized with the proposed revolt and "had evidently meddled in it, what she had done was of no dangerous consequence."

In reference to the fines to be paid by the transgressors, he had bidden him "make the chiefest of Long Finn's accomplices forfeit half their goods and chattels. The less guilty shall pay a fine in proportion as they are more or less guilty; the ordinary people are not to be too much frighted, but are to be punished by taxes heavy enough to keep them too busy paying them to give attention to anything else."

Jan Stalcop, Juns Junstersen, Hindrich Collmann, Olle Fransen, were to receive "the mark," a branded R, on their faces. Stalcop and Junstersen must each pay fifteen hundred guilders, Fransen two thousand guilders, Collmann nine hundred and thirty guilders.

The dreaded brand! Was Gunnar's face to have imprinted upon it by a red-hot iron that hideous disgraceful mark? His sentence was not yet pronounced. Astrid and her mother covered their eyes and shuddered; Lars felt his soul cringe before that frightful possibility.

But mercy was shown him in this, perhaps because of his youth. The punishment meted out to him was a fine only. Yet it was so heavy! Fifteen hundred guilders. Lars groaned aloud, for it was he, Gunnar's father, who would have to pay.

"It will ruin me altogether," he told himself under his breath. "I can never do it."

Notwithstanding, he was immeasurably thankful that Gunnar would not have to bear the brand. And Astrid and Ingeborg reminded themselves of this over and over; they scarcely heard the rest of his sentence, the staggering amount of the fine, in the rush of their relief that he was not to be branded. Not until later would they grasp it and be weighed down by the consciousness of what it was to mean to Lars, and to them all, when it came to paying a sum so great.

Gunnar was sent away from the bar to liberty. He came, sick at heart, ashamed, his head upon his breast. He felt that he could not look his world in the face, least of all those who loved him.

Lars would not have it so. His hand was quick to grasp his repentant son's and wring it. "Look up, my boy," he bade him manfully. "Whatever is to be met, we will meet together."

"To think that I should have brought this upon you by my folly and disobedience," mourned Gunnar, his voice shaking.

"Come, come," said Lars, "you must let that rest. Have I not told you that before? Here we are now, your mother, Astrid, Karin, Kirsten, all glad to have you back among us." He shoved him gently toward

Ingeborg, who drew down the lad's head to kiss him tenderly.

Then Astrid must have her turn. The twins also, shrieking gleefully, "Gunnar! Gunnar!"

Eric, who had been wedged in by the crowd on the opposite side of the Court Room, saw them reunited. It was he who had found Gunnar, he who had served his good friends, and above all, Astrid. The knowledge warmed his heart. It was true that Gunnar had received a sentence that would be a heavy burden upon him and upon his father for years to come, but he was to be at home, and his eyes opened at last. At home and free.

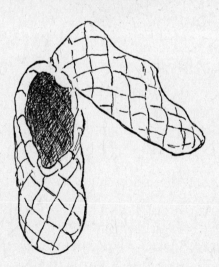

CHAPTER XXI

Juffrou Armgart Printz mounted her bay mare and rode forth from Printz Torp.

A long woolen cloak lined from top to bottom with brown squirrel, a squirrel cape and hood and gloves protected her from the bitter cold of the

December morning. The hoofs of her mare rang on the frozen ground.

Old Olga peered after her from the kitchen window.

"Juffrou goes to see the Long Finn whipped on the Market Plaine in New Castle," she observed to Olle who was greasing his boots by the fire.

"And to see how the mark becomes him, no doubt," grunted Olle from his low stool. "It will spoil his looks for good and all."

Olle had no looks to spoil, and thought small things of those who had. He dipped his clumsy fingers in the melted tallow and went on stolidly greasing his cowhide boots.

"He came here often," remarked Olga.

"And for no good," replied Olle. "He has turned out to be a rogue."

"Now that it is known that he is a liar as well as a rogue, our mistress rides to see how he takes his punishment."

"She was smart enough to keep her own skirts out of the fire," contributed Olle, "even though she believed him at first."

"Trust her for that," mumbled Olga.

Olle and Olga had observed far more than Armgart Printz had supposed.

She trotted on, unaware of how well these servants of hers understood her.

No one went from Lars Nilsson's house to the Market Plaine that morning. The little family knew what was to be done at the whipping post on the Market Plaine. Unlike many of the people living in those days, they had no relish for such spectacles. They remembered also that their own Gunnar might have been made to endure public flogging. That thought was sufficient to cause them to shun the Market Plaine until Long Finn had been taken from it.

Not so the mass of inhabitants of New Castle. Folk were wont to flock to public punishments as to a curious sight. Children young enough to be led by the hand were taken, too, to warn them of what lay in store for evildoers.

Armgart Printz found the Market Plaine thronged by young and old when she drew rein at the edge of it.

She did not dismount. She could see better from horseback, and she wished to see. Long Finn had lied to her, had tried to make a fool of her. She bore him a deep resentment for it, and believed that because he had deceived her, he deserved to suffer.

The whipping post rose stark and grim on the

Market Plaine. A space was kept cleared around it, and a lane open for passage to the post of the culprit and he who was to wield the whip.

A sudden craning of necks, an excited hum of voices told that Long Finn was coming.

Armgart Printz saw him sooner than those of the crowd who were on foot. Her eyes followed him steadily as he advanced. They hardened when he reached the whipping post, and she beheld the dark red brand upon his ashen cheek and the huge inscription fastened to the breast of his coat.

His features were set as in an iron mold. He looked neither to right nor left. With unfaltering step and scornful bearing he had come. Scornful in his fetters he held himself now.

They stripped him to the waist and his back was naked to the icy air.

They bound him to the post, his face inward.

The crowd leaned forward as the whip was raised, shrank away as the lash hissed through the air and fell on Long Finn's flesh.

Not a sound burst from him then, nor under any of the heavy strokes that followed. By superhuman effort, by indomitable pride, he neither screamed nor groaned, though every stroke cut deep into and tore quivering muscles, beat upon anguished nerves, and brought the blood in streams.

Forty lashes were given him and that part of his ordeal was over. His upper garments were dragged on again and his keepers took him away. He staggered as he walked, but his body was held rigidly erect as though it were made of steel.

The onlookers marveled that in his agony of fiery pain he managed to accomplish this.

Armgart Printz regarded him unmoved.

Long Finn's head was lifted determinedly even in this bitter moment of his disgrace and shame. He perceived Armgart Printz, proud and safe, seated high above him on her bay mare.

Their eyes met and they exchanged a farewell glance. In hers were icy scorn and studied indifference to his sufferings. In his were fiery disdain, hatred, contempt. Their dealings with one another had been in secret and unwitnessed. He dared not accuse her of aught for lack of proof.

Without a syllable he passed on to the crowning miseries of his sentence.

She sat secure and arrogant as ever she had—the "proud lady of Tinicum."

The gruesome spectacle was ended and the populace began to scatter to their business or to their homes.

Juffrou Printz composedly took the road to Printz Torp.

Hans Brikker ambled to the tavern to wet his throat. He had gloated over every cruel stroke of the lash as it descended upon the culprit. He had not gone to the scene to learn a lesson from the hideous sight of the flogging, but to indulge his inhuman instincts instead. It would have pleased him beyond measure if he could have seen a like punishment inflicted upon Gunnar Nilsson.

Since that was not to be, he reflected with huge satisfaction upon the ruinous fine imposed upon Gunnar which, by unremitting toil on his part and his father's, the youth must strive to pay. That would take years. The thought of this was sweet to Brikker, rolling it over in his mind while he quaffed strong thick beer in the taproom of the tavern.

Gunnar, sharpening tools at the grindstone in the storehouse that morning, thought of it too with bitterest self-condemnation. What would he not give if only he could wipe out the madness and wild rebellion of the past few months; if only he could see his father relieved of the harassing undeserved burden that had fallen upon his shoulders; if only he could see his mother's face serene and carefree as he had known it before Long Finn came to cast a baleful influence; if only he could see his dear Astrid smile brightly once more.

How much he owed them all! And how much he owed to Eric, who had sought him and been the first to bring him to his senses! How was he to earn money for the fine? He must hunt and trap for furs, must trade with the savages for more.

Lars at his workbench in the kitchen pondered the same problem diligently, incessantly. From the sale of his crops, by Gunnar's trapping and the sale of the pelts, the sum must be raised, but the fine could be paid only a very little at a time.

In the midst of his planning, Astrid deserted her work at the cheese press in the buttery and went to his side.

"Father," she said, "you know I am a good weaver and a good spinner for mother herself has taught me. I can earn money in that way and help to pay Gunnar's fine. Perhaps—" She paused doubtfully, and then went on, "Perhaps Juffrou Printz still wants her cloth woven by me here. That would bring money almost at once."

Ingeborg, mending a rent in Karin's petticoat, shook her head in swift negation. "No," she said decidedly.

Lars drew his lips into a grim line. "Spin, weave,

my daughter, for anyone else, but not for Armgart Printz. If the truth were known, she is probably almost as much to blame as Long Finn for the trouble that has fallen upon us."

"I will weave for others then, and I will go and seek them," replied Astrid.

Thus by unremitting industry and self-denial they planned to bear the burden of the fine together.

Influences were at work to try to lift at least a portion of the load from them, but with no success as yet. Peter Kock had stressed to Captain Carr the unvarying loyalty and honesty of Lars Nilsson, had called to Carr's notice again and again the youth and immaturity of Gunnar. His recommendation for mercy had seemed to fall upon barren ground. Carr told him that it would have a salutary effect upon all the young men in the settlements to make a conspicuous example of this particular youth. After several attempts to have the sentence lifted or modified, Kock found it best to say no more.

Philip Stanton was persistent, though with discretion. His sympathies were strongly stirred by an occasional glimpse of Astrid's troubled face when he encountered her in the village, or by her grave tones when she answered his friendly inquiries as to how she did. He felt for Lars. He understood Gunnar and took note of the valiant efforts he was making to redeem himself by accepting his responsibilities and leaving behind the rebellious carelessness of his earlier years. He saw him setting his traps, met him hunting fur-bearing animals in the woods.

December was more than half over. Long Finn had been sent in chains to New York to remain in prison in the Stadt House until the ship which was to convey him to Barbadoes was ready to sail.

The day after he had departed from New Castle, Stanton spoke once more for Gunnar. "If you would only let him have the chance to go free into life," he pleaded earnestly, "I am convinced he will never transgress again. He is really a fine fellow, sound at heart, and he has learned his lesson."

He said this over a tankard of ale in the taproom of the tavern.

Carr raised his ale to his lips and cast him an amused glance over the rim of his mug. "You are like your father, Philip," he replied. "He was always trying to persuade me to mildness with culprits. What would become of law and order if I yielded in season and out of season to men like him and you?"

"This once," begged Stanton. "You will not lose by it. You will never regret it. Nor will His Majesty lose, if this lad is given the chance to start life again without a halter around his neck."

He checked himself abruptly for he detected a hint of impatience creeping into Carr's face. He must not cut off all hope of clemency in the future by being too insistent now.

Carr answered his appeal testily. "I'll think of it, but I make no promises, Philip." And then he promptly changed the subject.

CHAPTER XXII

HANS BRIKKER WAS PUR-
suing a stealthy course through the forest.

He had discovered the location of all Gunnar
Nilsson's traps, and at this early hour of the morning
he was visiting them before Gunnar should arrive to
gather up his catch.

Brikker was resolved that Gunnar should find
every one of these carefully made and set traps rifled
and broken. That was a form of revenge upon the

Nilssons that he might often taste, and if he used proper caution he need not be found out. The blame for the loss of animals and damaged traps could easily be attributed to roving savages or to those who lived in the neighborhood of Tinicum.

To avert suspicion from himself and fix it upon some unknown Indian, Brikker wore moccasins. Gunnar would see the footprints and would suppose the theft had been committed by one of those who had heretofore been his firm friends.

Slung over Brikker's back were his boots and the bodies of several small animals obtained from Gunnar's traps. When he had visited all the traps, he would change his moccasins to his boots at some favorable spot.

So far as the animals were concerned, he could march boldly with them to his own door in broad daylight, for he, like many others in New Castle, did a little trapping and hunting on his own account during the season. Hence no one would think of him as the thief. Lars and Gunnar might suspect him, but unless they caught him in the act of robbing a trap, they would not dare to accuse him.

A deep hush filled the forest. Bare twigs and tufted pine boughs etched themselves against a sky not yet flushed by the coming of the sun.

Brikker plodded along the snowy ground, highly pleased with what he had already accomplished and looking forward to richer spoils. He had excellent prospect of this for Gunnar was an unusually skillful trapper.

Safe from observation he seemed in that vast solitude through which he was moving cautiously. There was no mark upon the snow around him but footprints of bird or rabbit. There had been no sign of life around Lars Nilsson's house when he had slunk by it. None but himself was abroad apparently, either there or here. Yet he was sly and underhand by nature, and went warily even when he thought there was no danger.

Finally he came to a trap which had a fine mink in its toils. He halted to consider whether he should take it or not, for a mink pelt was considered of small value in those days. However, he could not reconcile himself to let Gunnar have the insignificant sum it would bring.

He knelt down clumsily to kill the animal and lift it from the trap.

A voice directly behind him startled him. The voice was sufficiently familiar, but he had not imagined that its owner was within miles of him.

He turned his head and saw Running Weasel,

wrapped in his blanket, grinning down upon him.

"My brother must want fur when he takes a mink," Running Weasel was saying, "though because it is the mink of his enemy, Gunnar Nilsson, he may not despise it."

Brikker looked black. Outside of being caught by either Gunnar or his father, nothing could have aggravated him more than to be detected in his thieving by Running Weasel, for it gave the savage the upper hand and he would not hesitate to use it.

Running Weasel made this evident before the Dutchman could reply.

"Perhaps," he continued, leering disagreeably, "my brother would not wish to have it known that he meddles with Gunnar Nilsson's traps. It might make much trouble for my brother."

Hans Brikker was only too well aware of this for, though Running Weasel should speak of it to none but red men, those were friends to Gunnar and they might not hesitate to do a mischief to anyone who injured him in any way.

Running Weasel continued craftily. "No doubt my brother does not wish to have me tell where it would harm him that Running Weasel has seen him stealing from these traps. Is that not so?"

Still Brikker did not speak. He was in a tight situation and was trying to think how he could extricate himself from it to his own advantage.

The savage meant to have the advantage entirely for himself. "If my brother would like to have Running Weasel hold his tongue," he went on relentlessly, "there is one thing that he can do."

Brikker did not need to be informed of what that was.

Nevertheless, Running Weasel continued to speak and with a distinct air of command. "Tonight my brother will bring to the place that he knows, plenty of 'firewater'—five times as much as he ever has before. If he does not, Running Weasel will tell everywhere what he has seen this morning."

Hans Brikker scrambled up from the ground, the dead mink in his hand. He brushed the snow from his knees. "Hold your tongue, then," he growled. "You shall have the 'firewater.'"

"Tonight?" demanded the savage.

"Tonight."

"In the place that my brother knows?"

"In that place."

The moon rose late that night. A couple of hours before its silver disk showed its rim above the horizon, Hans Brikker, armed with a large bottle of brandy, approached the rendezvous.

The Indian was crouched in the dark space between the two warehouses. Although he seemed to sleep, his senses were alert, and the instant Hans Brikker appeared at the opening, he rose as if on springs and thrust out an eager hand.

Brikker was not minded to let him have the brandy without a more binding assurance than Running Weasel's mere word that he would keep quiet about the traps. He must pledge himself by a belt of black and white wampum.

"I have brought the 'firewater' as I promised, but first you must give me a belt, a black and white belt, else you might forget that you are to say nothing about what you saw this morning in the forest by Gunnar Nilsson's trap."

Running Weasel replied angrily, "I do not need to give a belt of wampum. The word of Running Weasel is enough."

Hans Brikker insisted. "If Running Weasel is in earnest, he will give the wampum."

The Indian's eyes glinted dangerously. "The 'firewater' without the wampum," he demanded. He fingered his scalping knife, keen as a razor.

Brikker turned cold with fear. The spot was lonely. At this hour no one would come that way. The folk of the town were asleep in their barred and shuttered houses. Even the tavern, a good distance off, was closed. No one could hear him if he screamed for help, nor would he do so at the risk of having his villainies exposed.

He must give the brandy and trust to the future to furnish him with some hold upon the savage that would keep his lips sealed.

Slowly, reluctantly he produced the bottle of enormous size, containing the strongest brandy obtainable.

Running Weasel snatched it from him and poured the liquid in a fiery torrent down his greedy throat.

The Dutchman stood aghast at seeing this quantity, which should have lasted for days, swallowed in one mighty flood.

Well for him if he had not tarried to watch it, if his feet had not refused to perform their office for that brief moment.

The liquor mounted to Running Weasel's brain and crazed him. He threw down the empty bottle, seized Brikker, and shouted, "More."

Brikker shook his head. "I have no more."

"More, more," snarled Running Weasel, shaking the fat Dutchman like a leaf.

"I have no more," panted Brikker, struggling to escape. But terror had robbed him of strength. Madness from the great quantity of brandy he had drunk made Running Weasel murderously strong.

"More, more," he clamored viciously.

"Tomorrow," promised Brikker, his teeth rattling in his mouth.

"Tonight—now," persisted Running Weasel. One of his sinewy hands was at the wretched man's throat. The other threatened him with uplifted knife.

To obtain the brandy for him tonight was impossible. Brikker could only move his head helplessly from side to side. "The tavern is shut," he protested faintly. "I have no more."

Running Weasel in his frenzy failed to grasp the import of what Brikker said. He craved brandy now and was refused instant gratification.

Enraged beyond all bounds, he plunged the knife into the Dutchman's throat and cast him bleeding and gurgling to the frozen ground.

Brikker lay there, twitching convulsively.

Running Weasel stooped, ran his scalping knife deftly around Brikker's crown, removed the scalp and hung it to his belt.

The yells of a drunken savage as he raced through the town to the woods beyond it, roused few of the inhabitants to more than momentary consciousness. Those who woke told themselves that Gerritt the smith, who lived at the north end of New Castle, had ample reason for complaining that drunken savages in the woods near his house annoyed him so much that he might be forced to move elsewhere.

Running Weasel rushed on through the forest, and burst leaping and yelling into the camp of his tribe. In his wild ravings he boasted of the deed which he had just done, blabbed of how he had served Brikker in the past, how he had betrayed Long Finn and Hindrich Collmann.

His fury spent, he tumbled, drugged and senseless, into his lodge.

The chief men of his tribe held council together, smoking their pipes slowly and deliberately around a freshly kindled fire. They were indifferent to the fate of Long Finn, but for Hindrich Collmann they cared much. Treachery to him and to the tribe they would not forgive.

Before morning dawned they had made Running Weasel pay the penalty of his bad faith, and he had followed Hans Brikker into the hereafter.

At sunup, Eric Helm, on his way to the shore, passed the space between the warehouses where Brikker's lifeless body lay. By chance he looked casually into the narrow space. What he saw brought him to a dead stop. He gazed upon the awful sight, spellbound and dumb with horror. Then he began to run.

Five minutes later he was reporting at the fort what he had seen. Captain Carr, in the exercise of his authority, gave orders to have Brikker's body removed and buried.

Eric realized that he must tell Elsa next. He found her, a shawl over her head, looking out through the open door. A puzzled expression was on her face.

She called to Eric before he had time to address her. "Hans Brikker is not in the house! He has not been in all night! The door was not locked nor barred. When I came into the kitchen just now, I found that his bed has not been slept in. The door he always closes and fastens himself when he comes in. This is all very strange. It has never happened before."

Eric answered her quietly. "He will not come home, Elsa."

"Not come home?" she echoed, uncomprehending.

"Never again. He is dead. An Indian killed him last night, down by the warehouses."

"Hans Brikker—dead!" stammered Elsa, scarcely believing her ears.

"Dead," repeated Eric. "I saw him there, and went and told the officer at the fort. Captain Carr has ordered his body to be taken away and buried."

Elsa stared at him helplessly. "Then they will not bring him here?" she managed to say presently.

"No."

She looked about her distractedly as though wondering what she was to do in the midst of these strange circumstances.

Eric came to her rescue. "And you, Elsa, must close the house at once, and go to the Orphan Master. He will decide what you are to do. Touch nothing in the house, then no one can say that you have meddled. Put on your cloak and head-shawl, lock the door, and I will go with you to the Orphan Master and tell him what has happened."

Elsa obeyed him without question. In shabby cloak and faded head-shawl, she left behind her the house in which she had suffered so much and been so unhappy, to follow her friend to the Orphan Master.

CHAPTER XXIII

Astrid WIPED HER EYES
with the corner of her red and green striped apron,
and leaning her forehead against the wall inside the
storehouse, sobbed aloud.

Christmas was at hand, a joyful season marked by
many quaint customs among the Swedes. Always
she had looked forward to it with keenest anticipation, prepared industriously weeks beforehand to
celebrate it. The customs would be kept as hereto-

fore. No one in the family would think of doing otherwise, but there was no prospect of the gay and carefree rejoicing that had been theirs in former years.

She was telling herself, while the tears trickled down her cheeks, that there was much to be thankful for. All the family were alive and well. Gunnar had become steady and dependable. They had food and clothing and a comfortable roof over their heads. But life went gravely, overshadowed by such cares and burdens they had never thought would be theirs.

No lack of courage, no lack of effort to be cheerful had been displayed by any member of the family. Astrid had borne her part bravely, had compelled herself to smile, had prayed night and morning that she would not fail in anything that might be of help and comfort to those she loved in this time of trial.

But now here was Christmas and the memory of past happy Christmases flooded in upon her. She was alone in the storehouse and could indulge herself in the tears which streamed out in spite of all she could do.

From the wood the sound of Gunnar's ax broke crisp and sharp upon her ears. He was chopping spruce branches. These, finely cut, were to be strewed over the kitchen floor.

Gunnar had done well with his trapping except for that one exasperating morning when he had gone to his traps and found half of them robbed and broken. He had guessed correctly that this was Brikker's spiteful work, and became convinced of it when they were left unmolested after his sudden death.

In her mind's eye Astrid could see her father at his workbench, fashioning with solemn care the great straw cross which was to be fastened outside the house door.

Already crosses had been painted on all the barrels, troughs, and other vessels to drive away evil spirits. For the same reason steel had been placed on the barndoor and in the barn. That night the cattle's teeth must be rubbed with salt. No foot must tread within the stable at midnight to see the animals kneel and hear them speak.

The Swedes and Finns were a superstitious people, and still believed in ghosts, giants, gnomes, and evil spirits lurking about to do mischief. They firmly believed in witchcraft, too, and that Finns, in particular, could work magic and sorcery.

Long Finn, fettered in his cell in the Stadt House, cursed his lot at this season. Armgart Printz, "proud lady of Tinicum," cared little whether Christmas was kept at Printz Torp or not. Old Olga and Olle could follow the ancient Swedish customs if they chose. As for herself, she had escaped exposure and disgrace, that was enough for her.

In New Castle the English were preparing to celebrate in their own way, the Dutch in theirs, the Swedes and Finns in theirs.

In Lars Nilsson's house, Ingeborg was baking the special "Christmas bread." Special beer had been brewed days ago for drinking the Yule Skoal together on Christmas Eve.

All at once Astrid was smitten by remorse. Here she stood weeping while everyone else was making ready for the sacred day. She remembered that the sheaves of wheat and rye had not yet been made and fastened to poles for the birds that they might not hunger on Christmas nor during the cold days that would follow. How the birds would flock to these sheaves, plucking out the fat kernels with their bills.

She dried her eyes quickly and started toward the barn. The afternoon sun was in her eyes, and she could scarcely see Eric Helm who was coming up the path bearing two tall poles on his shoulders. Splendid generous sheaves of wheat and rye were bound to the poles, thick with plump grains. He was bringing them as his special Christmas offering to Astrid, for he knew how dearly she loved the birds.

"I hope I am in time," he called to her, "so that you need not make any sheaves yourself. If you say so, I will set these poles up for you. Our wheat and rye are extra fine this year."

"On each side of the house door," she begged, when she had exclaimed delightedly over the gift and praised the size of the grains. "Then we can see the birds from the kitchen windows as they fly to the poles and eat."

He did as she wished and planted the poles firmly, each upholding its rich burden.

"Mother will want to speak to you, Eric," she said when he had finished. "I heard her saying that you and your father must come tonight as you always have, to eat the Christmas porridge and drink the Yule Skoal with us."

Eric went into the house, received Ingeborg's warm invitation, and gave the promise that he and Anders would be there at dusk.

Gunnar brought in the spruce and scattered it thickly over the kitchen floor like a green carpet. Astrid helped him to distribute it evenly.

He did not once raise his head. Astrid noticed that his face was working painfully, and that he bit his lips hard as though he were making a strong effort to control his feelings.

When the last bit of spruce had been thrown down, he hurried to the log stair which led to the loft overhead and stumbled up it.

Astrid's heart was filled with sympathy for him. She waited a few moments, whispered to her mother, and then followed him.

She found him on his knees by his bed, his head buried in the covers, his shoulders shaking.

She knelt down beside him and threw her arms around him. "Gunnar, our dear Gunnar," she said gently, "do not grieve so."

"Why should I not grieve?" he asked despairingly, his voice smothered in the bedclothes. "I have brought trouble upon my father, upon every one of you. I deserve punishment; I earned it. But the rest of you, who are blameless, are suffering and will suffer because of me. If only I knew some way, however difficult for me, to pay this fine entirely myself, it would not be so bad. That my father and mother and you are paying for my misdeeds—oh, Astrid, I cannot bear it."

Astrid stroked his bowed head lovingly. "Take heart, Gunnar, our own Gunnar. Are you not ours? Should not we, who love you so dearly, help you in this? Help you, too, to be your finest self? Ah, we will do it gladly. We shall lift our heads in pride of you some day, because of what you have become through the very hardship of this trial."

She said this to him with a wisdom and foresight beyond her years, inspired to it by his deep need.

Her words brought a measure of comfort to his sore spirit, gave him courage to rise from his knees, to return to the kitchen, to go to Lars and help him carry out the finished cross of straw and fasten it to the outside of the house door. When that was done, he assisted him in fetching in the immense Yule log, cut that morning.

Astrid brought forth the large candles and put them in candlesticks. These were the Christmas candles. Her mother's silver brooch and earrings, her own silver necklace, some of the Sunday clothes of the family would be laid where the light from the candles would fall upon them. That would bring good luck.

She was in the midst of this when Elsa ran in, her round countenance beaming, her gray eyes dark and sparkling with excitement.

"Think, only think," she cried, scarcely able to contain herself, "I am to have a place in the Orphan Master's own house, to serve his wife, a good kind woman! Oh, that such splendid fortune should come to me!"

"None deserves it more," exclaimed Astrid, embracing her.

"None indeed," declared Ingeborg warmly.

"I go there tonight," panted Elsa. "On Yule Eve!"

"That blesses your good fortune," Ingeborg told her.

When Elsa left, Astrid returned to her duties, filled with a glow of unselfish satisfaction that such well-merited happiness had befallen her friend.

While she worked she reminded herself of what her father had said quietly to his family a week ago in referring to Christmas: "We must do everything exactly as usual. Because we have hardships to bear in our lives is no reason why we should not pay honor with thankful hearts in the old way to Him who gives us every good gift and strength to meet whatever comes."

When night fell the spacious kitchen was redolent of the odor of the freshly cut spruce warmed to delicious fragrance by the heat streaming from the enormous Yule log in front of the chimney back.

Karin and Kirsten picked up spruce twigs from the floor, sniffed them ecstatically, and held them to each other's nose.

The pot of Christmas porridge, rich with milk and butter, dangled smoking from the crane. The Christmas bread in generous slices was heaped high in the best dish. The best linen cloth, beautifully embroidered by Astrid, covered the well-scoured table. The best painted and carved bowls, spoons, and mugs were ranged upon it in order.

Anders and Eric strode in, their ears and cheeks scarlet with cold, their fingers tingling in spite of their thick woolen mittens.

The Yule supper was ready to be eaten.

Guests and family were gathering round the table when there came a knock on the door.

Astrid opened it.

On the sill stood Philip Stanton, fine in his great broadcloth cloak lined and elegantly trimmed with fur. The jewel which clipped his feather to his beaver hat glistened richly where the light from the Christmas candles struck it.

"That will bring luck to him," thought Astrid, as she stepped aside, inviting him to enter.

Stanton went straight to where the others were gathered round the table, his handsome face bright with generous friendliness.

"A Christmas blessing on this house and all in it," he said blithely, flinging back his cloak.

"And on yourself, sir," spoke Lars.

"I bring good news," continued Stanton.

"Good news?" whispered Astrid, stealing closer, her lips parted, her pulses beating fast.

"Good news?" repeated Lars and Ingeborg, wondering what it could be.

"Good news?" thought Gunnar soberly, not daring to believe that there could be good news for him.

Anders and Eric threw swift glances at one another, not guessing what Stanton meant.

"The very best," announced Stanton, smiling. "Captain Carr allows me to bring you word that because of Gunnar's youth and his recent good behavior, the fine is to be lifted, lifted altogether. Not a single guilder, not a single penny is to be paid."

The room spun round for Gunnar, the floor seemed to rise up from under his feet. He caught dizzily at the edge of the table to steady himself, to save himself from falling. This sudden unexpected release from grief and despondency, this sudden lifting of a crushing burden was almost too much for him. Emotion overmastered him altogether. He could not utter a word.

Lars went white to the lips. Never would he have dreamed that such a thing as Stanton had said could be possible.

Tears of joy rushed to Ingeborg's eyes and down her cheeks.

Into Astrid's face stole a dazzling radiance. Into her heart long troubled, into the hearts of those she loved, descended a great peace. Earnest prayers had been sent up day by day out of grief and pain for courage to shoulder burdens, bear responsibilities uncomplainingly and cheerfully. These had been answered tonight by a benefaction which they had never asked for, had never hoped for. God, in His goodness, had stirred human instruments to mercy. Gunnar was pardoned. Gunnar was to have his chance.

Incense-like, inaudibly, their thanks and praise for

this rose to the Giver of every good.

"Gunnar—free!" breathed Astrid, breaking the profound stillness.

"Free, my son," cried Lars exultantly, laying his hand on Gunnar's shoulder.

"And you, oh, father, you are free," returned Gunnar, finding his voice. "You, who have deserved nothing but the best, are free!"

Astrid at Stanton's side spoke softly. "You have persuaded Captain Carr to do this for Gunnar, for us. No one need to tell us that, sir."

"It was happiness to do it," replied Stanton sincerely.

Gunnar sprang forward now to pour forth his gratitude in impulsive words. Then Lars, then Ingeborg spoke theirs, while Karin and Kirsten, comprehending no more than that something good had befallen, danced up and down, and twirled upon their toes.

Anders and Eric, looking on, gripped each other's hands tightly to express their mutual satisfaction.

While Stanton was trying laughingly to make light of his own part in influencing Captain Carr's decision, Astrid ran to the carved and painted beakers, and filled them to the brim.

"Skoal!" she cried.

"Skoal, skoal!" shouted all, lifting the beakers to their hearts
in the ancient Swedish fashion

"Skoal!" cried Gunnar, handing them round.

"Skoal, skoal!" shouted all, lifting the beakers to their hearts in the ancient Swedish fashion and fixing their eyes on Philip Stanton before they quaffed.

"Skoal! Skoal! Skoal!" The Yuletide toast, loud and joyous, mounted to the rafters.

GERTRUDE CROWNFIELD was born in Baltimore, Maryland. Nearly all her early education was received at home and under private tutors. After teaching school for about ten years, she took up nursing in New York, graduating with honors. She worked side by side with a noted nerve specialist until his death, when she turned to writing. Most of her books have been of American historical background, written out of a love of history and a deep desire to make it live for young people, stirring them to love of country and true patriotism.

AGNES LEHMAN was born in Buffalo, New York. She graduated from Syracuse University, and later studied illustration at the Art Students' League in New York. For several years she specialized in illustrating books for children and the teen age. Then followed travel abroad to little known towns in the British Isles, Germany, France, Holland, et cetera, which resulted in her writing books for children also. She looks forward to the time when the world is again at peace and she can travel to faraway places.